JURASSIC

Jurassic

Michael Bertolini

Published by Michael Bertolini, 2024.

JURASSIC

MICHAEL J BERTOLINI

JURASSIC

First edition. June 1, 2024.

Copyright © 2024 Michael Bertolini.

ISBN: 979-8224166930

Written by Michael Bertolini.

To fans of dinosaurs everywhere

FLIGHT 19

Five bombers painted a shade of blue that resembled sea water cast shadows on the ocean's waves. The men, each experienced, were confident when they set out for the day. Even though a storm was brewing and there were clouds in the sky, the training was going to continue as scheduled.

Powers squinted as the five bombers approached a wall of clouds that wasn't supposed to be present on their course. There was a flash of lightning but no rumble of thunder. He gulped in fear though none of the other pilots could hear. Powers felt something strange and he was uncomfortable with entering the white emptiness.

The other four bombers were parallel to him on his port wing, though Powers never glanced at them or their single pilots. It was a training mission and he hoped to pass the exercise regardless of any odd event.

A voice that Powers didn't recognize, not one of the pilots that he'd come to know, came over his radio in a broken voice. The radio hissed which the device shouldn't have been able to do. "What're your compass readings?" Powers frowned.

"I don't know where we are, we must've got lost after that last turn." A voice, eerily similar to Power's own voice, whispered. Powers briefly glanced in the direction of the other bombers but the pilots all appeared too focused to ask Powers, just another student in the exercise, for help.

"This is FT-74, plane or boat calling 'Powers' please identify your self so someone can help you." FT-74 was the nearest bomber to Powers, another student by the name of Cox. Both pilots waited, Powers on the edge of his seat, but no reply came. The only voices were those from the other pilots, including Taylor who was leading the exercise.

"This is FT-74, plane or boat calling 'Powers' please identify your self so someone can help you." Cox tried again but no response was forthcoming. Cox then turned his attention to Taylor, FT-28. "FT-28, this is FT-74, what is your trouble?" Powers knew what Cox referred too; none of the students understood why the course was still due-East while turning to the West would lead to either Florida or Texas.

"Both my compasses are out," Taylor replied with some hesitation, "and I'm trying to find Fort Lauderdale, Florida. I am over land, but they are broken." Powers gulped again as the clouds flashed with interior lightning. "I'm sure that it's the Keys, but I don't know how far down and I don't know how to find Fort Lauderdale."

The clouds thinned and a shadow moved.

PART ONE
EARTH

1

John Deacon stood in the back of the massive yet sparse room, inches away from the pseudo-glass wall. He was looking out at the city stretched beneath him. Towering structures in varied hues of bronze glinted under the sun as clouds wafted through the canyons of steel.

On the 684th floor, John was above the rail lines that snaked through the city and connected people to their destinations in other parts of the city.

It was called the 'White City' on paper but most people had more colorful names to describe the city. White was a color none of them used. Pure and innocent; those two words could never be used to describe a city of such decadence.

People shuffled like ants along the walkways between the buildings. No matter what section of the sewers the ants came from, they were all eager to get whatever scraps that were thrown their way. John could hardly distinguish the ants from their surroundings; everything was dull and gray.

The pink sky filled the windows with rosy fingers as fluorescent lighting automatically clicked on in various parts of the city. The White City stretched from its northern reaches in old Massachusetts all of the way south to its terminal just south of the Atlanta Ruins.

"Do you want to tell me about it?" John hardly made any visible acknowledgement. Doctor Andrea Holloway sat in the center of the couch in the middle of the room. She crossed her legs and chewed on a pencil. John didn't really care; he wasn't going to pay any attention to Doctor Holloway. He was only going to the psychologist because of the accident.

It was an accident.

That was what John had put on all of his reports. They'd accidentally entered an unsecured area, even though the intelligence reports indicated that the area was safe. They'd accidentally been fired on by enemy insurgents, even though there were no enemy insurgents in the area.

They'd accidentally been killed.

The military docs hadn't liked what John had to say; the commanders gave John a medical discharge due to his 'accidental' injuries. That was almost a year gone by and little had been done. It was no miracle to fix a human face; and he'd have been fixed if the military docs hadn't patched John so quickly and horrifically.

Now there was a risk of infection; the wound could never be properly fixed without major surgery. Combat pay couldn't afford that level of surgery. John knew that he was damned to remain as he was for the remaining years of his mortal life.

If something didn't happen soon, John would be sure to keep that time short.

"Do you want to tell me about it?" Doctor Holloway asked again. Her voice remained calm as the setting sun crossed her light face. Her auburn hair was mimicked by the sun for an instant before the automatic drapes closed. John was forced to step away from the glass as vinyl strips fell in place.

"If it pleases the court," John turned his left eye toward Doctor Holloway, "I'd like this session to be over."

"That's always your choice, John," Doctor Holloway sighed and rose to her feet, "but remember, the longer that you resist my help only extends the period of time that you have to remain out of service." It was the duty of every White City citizen to enlist in the city military for a period of at least four years. That was the law; there were no draft dodgers because it was no draft.

Everybody served; nobody quit.

Soldiers like John enlisted of their own frcewill. They were aware that their lives belonged to the White City and they were accepting of that fact, ready to die in another civil war. Others were forced to serve. Anyone forced to serve was often heckled by the enlisted soldiers and given nicknames like 'fudge-packer' and 'snowball.'

John wanted to go back and serve the remainder of his mortal days. He loved the feeling of combat. He loved the way he stank in uniform. He loved the feel of oil leaking from the springs in the weaponry. He loved every aspect.

He just needed to get the medical ban lifted.

"Am I ever goin' to have a normal life?" John casually asked without looking directly at Doctor Holloway.

"What part of a normal life do you want?" Doctor Holloway asked. "You have no skills that can be used in the workforce, you have no higher learning, and you're injured." It was blunt but it was the truth.

"I want the part that gives me dreams."

"What do you dream about?"

"I dream of returning to battle," John finally walked closer to Doctor Holloway but sat in a chair before he reached her, "I dream of a soldier's life."

"Like the one you had?" Doctor Holloway spun the pen in her fingers like a baton.

"Exactly like that."

"Do you know what you'd have to do to achieve that?"

"There'd be extensive radiation treatment," John nodded, "I'd probably die." He shrugged; he'd made his mind on that matter long ago.

"At least you're aware." She sighed and glanced down at her notepad. John rubbed his face with his hands and could feel the scar tissue; the sickle-shaped scar ran from his forehead to his chin and passed through the remains of his right eye.

It was an accident that he survived when so many died.

"Can you write me a prescription?" John asked dryly. He looked at Doctor Holloway for a moment before looking away.

"For what?" Doctor Holloway looked at John.

"The usual."

"Are you still having nightmares?"

"Are you asking as my doctor or as a human?"

"Both."

"Just get me the drugs." The doctor sighed and jotted some notes down. She looked at the closest wall for a moment; there was a poster of a cat hanging from a tree branch in the center of the wall. The caption of the poster read 'hang on' and Doctor Holloway tried to do just that every day.

"Come back tomorrow, John," Doctor Holloway looked over at John, "if you still can't sleep..." Her voice faded away as she shrugged her shoulders.

"What?" He stopped rubbing his face.

"Then I'll give you the prescription that you requested." She leaned back in her seat and John stood. He looked at Doctor Holloway for a moment but said nothing. Finally, after an eternity of silence, he nodded his ascent and walked to the door.

The session was over. Two hundred credits just disappeared from his bank account.

"I'll see you tomorrow." John mumbled.

"John?" Doctor Holloway remained seated as another thought came to her. John paused and turned to look at her. He raised his left eyebrow. "Try to stay sober."

2

John walked out of the towering building after descending more than a hundred floors in the building's high-speed elevator. The interior of the building was made of faux marble and the carpeting was imported from another region of Earth; John didn't know where but no war was likely happening in that corner of the globe just yet. Since the White City was at peace with few countries, there weren't many options.

The lobby had meticulously maintained fake ferns decorating the corners while holo-mags depicting smiling people and half-naked women rested untouched on scattered tables.

When John pushed the doors open so that he could walk outside, he was hit by the late day sun and a brief haze. He had to shield his face in shadow as he walked from the building, a hundred paces down a fifty foot long walkway flanked by more fake plants, to the cracked general walkway that passed in front of the building. He turned to the left as his black jacket fluttered in the light breeze and scattered lights buzzed on.

Doctor Holloway's office was situated in the 'bronze' district. Most of the buildings had offices for psychologists, lawyers, and financial workers. The people that worked in that district could afford to live in either the 'gold' or 'blue' residential districts. Most of the population, including John, lived below the clouds in the massive 'gray' district that dominated the city. Fully 99% of the population lived in poverty, nowhere to go but the 'gray' district.

A train track running parallel to the walkway rumbled as a train sped by black like a bullet while reflecting the sunlight. The trains were the only mode of transportation in the city after vehicles were banned from the civilian sector. The trains were fast, gliding over rails at hundreds of miles per hour. John looked at the train but it moved so fast that he couldn't identify it. There was a chance that he'd have to take that train or one like it; he just had to walk to the nearest station.

There was a rumble in the sky and clouds moved in. John started to walk faster.

The walkway eventually started to curve away from the train track after nearly a mile of walking. Once the walkway had moved a short distance away it split in half. John went left, going down a dozen steps to the train station that was built under the general walkway. The stations in all of the nicer districts were kept clean and patrolled by flying robotic police sentries and their human counterparts: peace officers.

"Hey, watch where you're goin'!" A gruff voice snapped. John, who had been lost in thought, nearly walked into a peace officer, a man in plastic white body armor with a blank plate over his face to obscure his identity. Nobody really liked peace officers so nobody advertised themselves.

The Peace Officer had a black shock-stick that was clutched to his side in a tight fist. It crackled with unseen electricity.

A robot, the size of a small dog, hovered nearby. The robot had a red lens on its 'nose' and a pair of rotating wings that allowed it to hover. A small gun on a swivel rotated at John momentarily and then quickly moved away. The robot scanned John with a invisible light from its lens to identify him before flying away.

"Sorry." John knew better than to upset a peace officer. They may have been responsible for the security of the city, stationed in strategic places, but at a chaotic cost. Peace officers were known for their brutality and racism.

The peace officer looked at John for a moment before letting the damaged soldier pass; the angry peace officer slowly put the shock-stick back in the holster on his waist. John said nothing else and bowed his head in silent respect.

The station spread under the general pedestrian walkway and another set of steps led back up away from the enclosed terminal. An iron gated wall with a half-dozen silver gates on pneumatic hinges dominated the space between the main terminal and the tracks beyond; the entire terminal appeared very sterile and utilitarian. There was another rumble as a trained moved into the terminal. All trains, other than express, stopped at every terminal they reached. John waved his ID card in front of the scanner and the gate allowed him to go up to the train terminal.

Five credits just disappeared from John's bank account; his monthly VA check was quickly running away.

John managed to reach the train just before rain began falling through the open holes above the tracks. It wasn't normal rain; acid fell from the sky in torrents that were murderous to the homeless. The acid rain, an effect of the nuclear civil war that had wrecked the country, beat on the windows like drums as John found a seat on the train. He sat alone, the right side of his face close to the glass. His trench coat fell beside him as he crossed his legs and tried to relax even though he knew that the train was far from comfortable.

The doors slid shut and the train sped out of the station. John took a deep breath of recycled air and slowly released it. He closed his left eye and contemplated sleep; all that he had to do was find a comfortable position. But before he could do anything, he was aware that someone was very close to him. John's left eye slowly opened and he turned his head to see a man in an expensive suit sitting across from him. The man had a square jaw shaved to military perfection and eyes as cold as steel.

"Are you John Deacon?" The man asked.

"I was tryin' to sleep." John said and looked at the advertisements on the ceiling. He wasn't interested in body-cream for women but it was better than looking at the suit.

"Are you John Deacon?" The suit asked again. John sighed and looked at the man.

"That depends on who's asking." John said softly.

"I'm with NASA." John was impressed; the suit didn't show any emotion, that was a sign that the trait that had been trained out of him by extensive military training.

"Impressive." John mumbled. NASA was once just a space agency until it expanded. Deep space exploration had revealed possible hostile entities that NASA had become determined to eliminate. Thinking of that always made John laugh; hostile wasn't enough to describe the wrath possessed by the Githraki aliens.

"You come highly recommended to us." The suit said as he held out a badge for John to see. John looked at the circular badge with a ten-pointed star engraved within. The phrase 'Silent-Secure-Secret-Safe' was inscribed in the bronze star. The man said that he was from NASA but that didn't mean that NASA had sent him.

"You've been talking to the wrong people."

"We don't talk to the 'wrong people.'"

"That's true," John grinned, "if that badge is real."

"It's real." Falsifying those badges was one of the highest crimes in the city; anyone trying to pretend that they represented the council was asking for a death sentence.

"What's this about?" John knew that it was pointless to avoid the issue; the suit would get whatever information he was after.

"Afghanistan."

"Shit," John's head fell back, "what do you want to know?"

"You led a group of your fellow soldiers into an area that you knew to be dangerous-" John noted that the suit didn't answer the question.

"Intel said that it was safe," John's head snapped up and he looked at the suit, "we weren't prepared for combat."

"You knew it to be dangerous."

"I suspected that it was dangerous; there's a difference." John admitted with a sigh.

"The soldiers still followed you."

"We all went in but I was the only one to get out." John remembered the screams of pain.

"You were still injured." John shrugged.

"Shit happens."

"Did you see your attacker?" John sat in silence for a few minutes; if he didn't want to discuss this with the shrink, there was no way he would talk to the suit.

"That doesn't matter."

"I'm curious."

"You guys probably know," John sighed, "you guys would definitely know."

"You were brave," the suit said as he nodded, "and you've remained loyal to the military."

"Once a soldier, always a soldier." John yawned. The train approached one of the city hubs; massive towers that all trains were connected to. The city was built around the hubs and the train tracks snaked out like the spokes of a wheel. John had to disembark at the hub and make his way to another train. He lived in the region that was once part of Massachusetts while Dr. Holloway's office was above the ruins of New York City; even with the high speed trains, travel was still over an hour.

"We'd like to have someone of your caliber." The suit put his badge away.

"Get me reinstated," John said, "that'll help." He knew that *they* had the power.

"I'm talking about doing something bigger. Haven't you ever imagined going to a place that you've never experienced before? I'm not talking about a dustbowl warzone; I'm talking about a *very* different world where your skills can be of particular use. You were once a skilled soldier and a... man... of your caliber would be needed in such a place."

"Oh? What place would that be?"

"ICARUS." John blinked several times; he was unsure if he heard the suit correctly.

"What did you say?"

"The ICARUS Project could use you."

"Are you convinced that my service in Afghanistan is reason enough?"

"Personally," the suit shrugged, "no. I think healthy soldiers with perfect records are best for this job. Washed-up soldiers like yourself need traditional rehab, not some glorified chance at redemption."

"I suppose that the decision wasn't yours to make."

"No; the council has made it clear: get John Deacon to ICARUS." Many of the government agencies took their orders from the mysterious council that had replaced the Presidency.

"What about my injury?" It was impossible to ignored the damage inflicted to his face.

"Don't worry about it," the suit whispered, "what do you say?"

"I don't know," John said.

"You can make a real difference," the suit said, "the pay is good enough to afford the reconstructive surgery you need. If you want to go to a normal warzone..." His voice sounded as though he was trying to sell a new product in one of those commercials.

"I don't care about the money." That was a lie.

"If you want to get back into the service that you know," the suit was saying as the train moved into the hub, "surgery would be best."

"For someone that doesn't want me," John said, "you're selling the offer." He shook his head. The suit feigned a smile.

"I need an answer." The suit said as the train started to slow. John could hear the *thump* as the trained entered the hub.

"When?"

"Now." The suit jingled a few coins in his pocket, partially absent from the conversation.

"No," John said, "let me think on it first." He tried to look out one of the train windows but constant graffiti had forced the WC-Transit to whiten many of the glass panels permanently. John usually didn't care, there was little to see; but he didn't want to look at the suit any longer than necessary.

"Alright," the suit nodded and stopped playing in his pocket, "I have to change trains and get back to the office. Have an answer when I see you tomorrow." The train stopped, the doors opened, and the suit left without another word.

3

Night fell across the city as the storm moved away. John was in his small bedroom, deep in the bowels of the city, and wallowed in a tall glass of cheap liquor. He held a framed picture of Sarah, his late wife, and cried. He had married Sarah when he was young; perhaps too young. But they had been in love. When John learned that he would be deployed to Afghanistan, the two had married.

Sarah committed suicide after John's accident. False reports told her that the injury was fatal. Sarah, who believed in religion, felt that she'd be reunited with John in Heaven. John survived his injuries, Sarah died from an accidental drug overdose before she slit her wrists as planned.

Accidents haunted John.

"I was requested to join the ICARUS project," John said to the picture while drinking, "but I haven't made up my mind yet. The name, ICARUS, holds too much meaning and symbolism. Though, I suppose that DAEDALUS was not marketable." John had been lucky enough to study Greek Mythology in his younger years since Computer Sciences held no interest for him. "Icarus drowned when he attempted to flee Crete. He had wings made of feathers and wax but Daedalus, his father, instructed Icarus to avoid both the sun and the sea. The sun could melt the wax and the sea could take him. But Icarus didn't listen.

"Icarus was curious and in his excitement, he flew too close to the sun," John took another swig of his drink, "the wax melted and the feathers fell away. Icarus landed in the sea and drowned." John shook his head. "ICARUS is man's ambition." He put the picture down, on a small table beside the bed, and finished his drink.

He reached for the picture once he put the glass down but picked up the remote. The TV, a small square attached to the nearest wall, flicked on. The news, which John watched despite the censorship that plagued the media, was on but a commercial was playing.

"The adventure of a lifetime waits," a disembodied female voice was saying as swirling graphics moved around the planet, "for you. Register for your chance to go to ICARUS. Go to a new world unlike anything that you could ever imagine; colonists are needed." The screen changed.

"Now available, City-Card allows you to have money prepared when you need to travel on the train system through the city. Buy your card, load as much money on it as you want, and you're all set!" There was a young man in nice clothes on the screen, holding a plastic cube in one hand while talking animatedly with the other. "The City-Card is available at any hub location and select retailers."

"More shit to waste money on." John murmured even as he looked at his own City-Card; it had been required of him to accept his VA checks.

The screen changed to the glowing symbol of a cross. A whimsical light shone on the cross from above.

"Do you believe in God?" A disembodied male voice asked. "Does the thought of Heaven worry you or excite you? Does your soul need guidance or do you need to find true passion?" John shook his head. "The church of NuJesu wants you to join us! This Sunday morning, the church of NuJesu will be holding prayer in the fashion of the old religions. Pray for the souls of the lost, pray for the souls of the damned, pray for-" John clicked the TV off and put the remote back on the table. He finished his drink and decided to try to sleep.

4

"How're you feeling?" Doctor Holloway asked. She was again sitting on the couch while John sat in the chair across from her.

"Same shit," John shrugged, "as always."

"Did you get drunk again?"

"No." As far as he was concerned John hadn't been properly drunk in years; but that was debatable.

"Did you drink at all?"

"Some." John didn't bother lying about it.

"How much?"

"Six or seven glasses," John said, "whatever it took to help me sleep." Had it been the entire bottle?

"Why are you having trouble sleeping?"

"I had a lot on my mind yesterday."

"Like what?"

"I got a job offer," John said, "after I left your office. I'm wanted to join ICARUS."

"That's good," Doctor Holloway smiled.

"I'm still a cripple."

"I assume that ICARUS would change that."

"Yes," John said, "once I do a rotation..."

"You can afford to fix your face." She read his mind.

"Do you find it hard to look at my face?" John asked.

"No," Doctor Holloway admitted, "you're young and handsome."

"I'm thinking about going." John changed the subject.

"When would you depart?"

"I don't know," John shrugged, "but I doubt I'd wait long."

"So this could be your last session with me."

"Yes."

"If you complete a rotation without incident," Doctor Holloway said, "I'll sign the papers to get you back in active duty."

"I'd appreciate that."

"I'd still like to hear about your dreams." John shook his head and sighed.

"You just said that you'd clear me."

"I still want to know; what do you dream about?" John thought for a moment before looking at Doctor Holloway. "Do you think about the soldiers that died?"

"That's why I drink." John nodded.

"Do you remember their names?"

"I thought that you were supposed to help me get over this." He didn't answer the question because he didn't need too: Anderson, Cole; Emmerich, Oliver; Islander, Kate; Oleander, William; Underhill, Jason...

"Talking about it will help get you in the right direction."

"I'm not so sure that I want to talk about it."

"I think that you should."

"Let me ask you something," John turned his head away as he changed the subject, "I'm wondering about this mission and you approving me for active duty."

"What is it?" Doctor Holloway leaned forward in her seat.

"I'll be gone about sixty years or so," John said, "are you still going to be a therapist then?"

"How old do you think I am?" Holloway giggled and covered her face with her free hand.

"I'm assuming that you're in your late twenties like me." John wondered if Doctor Holloway had been forced to enlist in the military or if she had done it of her own free will; they had never discussed the topic.

"That's pretty close."

"I won't age in cryo-stasis. I won't be out of my thirties when I return and you'll be almost ninety."

"Were you going to make a point?"

"So how do I get reinstated?"

"I'll set a computer lock on your file," Holloway explained, "*if* you return with a clean record you'll automatically be reinstated." John took a deep breath but didn't say anything.

John departed Doctor Holloway's office. He'd likely never see her, or the inside of the building, again. He walked down the silent hall and entered the elevator.

As the elevator deposited John in the lobby; the sun struck him in the face. He put his sunglasses on as the rays, filtered by passing clouds, scanned the city like a digital scanner. John left the building and walked to the train station. He got onto the train and took the same seat that he'd taken the day before.

As promised, the suit was already waiting.

"So," the suit looked up as John sat down, "what's your answer?"

"I just have one question to ask you."

"Just one?"

"How long is the trip?" John asked and the suit smiled.

5

John opened his eyes and looked around. He was in a small box no larger than a coffin. If something had happened in flight, he'd have been ejected into the emptiness of space while the other people on the transport ship were none-the-wiser. But nothing had happened and John woke; the journey was nearing its completion.

The hydraulic door above his head opened and John slid out, strapped to a gurney. If not, he'd have floated away in the zero-g environment. The sound of the air pumps and opening doors filled the cavernous space as a medical team floated from person to person to inspect them.

A digital screen, a few inches above the opening of his coffin, clicked on automatically. A female, Asian with dark hair and slanted eyes, danced in front of a simulated background.

"Welcome to Jurassic Earth," the Asian dancer said in a crude voice that was obviously computerized, "it has been 23.6 years since departing Earth orbit. The time is oh-600." It was hard to imagine the scale of time when most of it had been done while sleeping. The transport had launched from a station between Earth and the Moon at nearly 29,000 miles per hour. The transport had traveled for over 11 years, propelled by the gravitational fluxes of the other planets in the solar system, before it even reached ICARUS. ICARUS was a ring that was constructed just past Pluto. It had to be far from Earth to avoid destroying the planet when it was active. ICARUS contained a simulated space-time worm hole that went back in time to a world that was more than 140 million years older than Earth. The transport went into the ICARUS gate, went back in time, and exited the ICARUS gate instantly. Then the transport had to travel to another space station built between Jurassic Earth and the Moon, another trip of over 11 years. The transport was just now attempting to dock with the space station. "A member of the medical crew will be to you shortly," the digital woman was saying, "once your straps are released, please feel free to use the facilities provided for you. It is recommended that you eat before departing the transport."

A man in a white jumpsuit floated over to John as the digital screen clicked off.

"Rise and shine!" The medical officer said with a smile. The medical team had been awake for a few days so that they could adjust to the environment. "How're you feeling?"

"Has it really been twenty-three years?" John asked.

"Twenty-three years and two-hundred nineteen days."

"Damn." John had a headache but he wasn't going to mention it unless asked. Most people that spent significant time in cryo-stasis suffered from either headaches or temporary amnesia. It was like having a hangover than kicked you in the balls.

"I'm going to release your straps one at a time," the officer said as he pressed the keys in a pad next to John's head, "I want you to slowly move around."

"I'm not a civilian." John said as his arms were released. He could feel the weightlessness grab hold of him instantly.

"Nobody is a civilian," the medical officer said with a laugh, "half of the people on this transport are active soldiers while the other half is comprised of inactive colonists that have already served in the military." The officer pressed more keys and John's chest and legs were released. John felt his body move away from the gurney.

A sharp needle pierced his skin and John cringed.

"What the fuck was that?" The language wasn't standard but soldiers on the battlefield were a law unto themselves.

"*Musculus Aedificator*," the officer explained as he slid the syringe back into his pocket, "it'll help you walk faster than if you sat in an isolation chamber for a month."

"How long until I can walk?"

"About an hour or so," the medical officer shrugged, "the station has artificial gravity."

"Why aren't you guys injected?" John asked as he took hold of the gurney to keep his body from moving far.

"Being able to float," the officer explained, "makes our job easier. Can you image us climbing ladders in this place?" He laughed before his voice became serious. "Get an M.R.E. and use the bathroom. Your body has been storing urine and feces for more than two decades."

"That's easy." John felt the need to piss.

"You're flagged in the system," the officer explained as he looked at a screen on his wrist, "which means that you have to go to the medical bay immediately upon arrival at the station."

"Why?" John frowned.

"If you're going to Earth," the officer pointed at John's face, "you'll need to take care of that wound or the planet will kill you." He sighed and pushed away from the gurney, moving on to the next person on his list. John watched him depart before going the opposite direction. The storage lockers, were the M.R.E.s were kept was not far, beyond those were the bathrooms.

The space station was cramped and utilitarian. Wires and cables hung along walls and ceilings while crew and visitors pushed past each other. The crew was accustomed to the artificial gravity which was intended to mimic that of Earth; but the visitors that just disembarked from the transport were still walking slowly.

"Watch it!" A man twice John's size spat as he pushed his way down the snaking corridor. The visitors, all dressed in gray jumpsuits with barcodes on their breasts, shuffled from the transport docks to the meeting hall on the far side of the station.

"Keep moving." John heard a familiar, female voice. He looked further down the corridor and saw the familiar face of Caroline West scanning every barcode and directing them through the station. Caroline had been under John's command a year before he left for ICARUS. She'd been transferred to the navy just months before the disastrous mission that cost John his right eye. Caroline was young, just over eighteen years old, with straight blonde hair and a thin body. Her curves, notably her breasts and ass, were accentuated by her utility belt around her waist and the v-shaped red sash she wore around her neck.

"Caroline?" John asked when he reached the end of the corridor. Caroline West scanned John's barcode and smiled when she saw the name.

"Sergeant Deacon," Caroline smiled perfect teeth, "It's been a long time."

"How's the navy?" The navy expanded into multiple areas once the Moon was colonized; they became a sea and space patrolling force. When ICARUS was built it was the navy that went through first.

"Same shit," Caroline shrugged, "as always."

"I was wondering where you were sent."

"Right after I left Afghanistan," Caroline said, "I was sent to ICARUS. I've been serving on this station ever since."

"Processing colonists seems boring."

"It's a temporary assignment," Caroline laughed, "this is my last gig before my rotation changes."

"Are you heading home?" John felt a twinge of jealousy; he wondered if the war in Afghanistan was still going on.

"See this sash?" Caroline flicked the red sash that she wore. "It means that I'm going to Jurassic Earth."

"I guess that I'm headed there."

"I'm going to be a squad leader," she explained, "and I'm checking the new arrivals to see who'll be under my command."

"Anyone interesting?" John asked. Caroline smiled and turned the screen she held so that John could see. John's ID information was displayed under a small heading: Deploy; West, Caroline.

"Am I reading this right?" John asked.

"I hope that you don't mind taking commands from a girl." She laughed.

"Girl, no. But you are younger than me."

"That depends on how you look at it," Caroline said, "in some ways, I'm older than you right now."

"How old are you?"

"It's not polite to ask," Caroline said, "but if you must know; I'm considered to be Thirty-three. The navy-only ships move faster than normal transports; my trip here was faster than yours."

"How old would you be if you remained on Earth?"

"Forty-two." She thought a few moments before answering as she did the math in her head.

"Nine years," John paused, "out of a ten-year rotation?"

"I could have gone back to our time and fulfill my rotational behind another desk, or I could complete another rotation on Jurassic Earth as a squad commander."

"I get it," John nodded, "you can't imagine a life outside of the military." John felt that way. Caroline nodded when her screen flashed red.

"Oh," she frowned when she looked at the screen, "are you alright?" She raised her thin eyebrows when she looked at John.

"Yes, why?"

"You're supposed to go to medical before the briefing meeting," Caroline noted the injury to John's face and understood the reason that her former commander needed medical attention, "take the corridor to the left and follow the signs." John nodded.

"I'll see you later." John said.

"You can call me 'commander' whenever you want." She smiled. John returned the smile and turned away; he walked to the medical bay alone and in silence.

6

The medical bay was spotless and showed no sign of complex wiring like the rest of the station. A nurse in blue scrubs looked up, her face partially hidden by a white mask.

"Can I help you?" She asked. Her brown eyes were all that was visible.

"I'm John Deacon," John said, "I was-"

"We're ready for you." The nurse pressed a button on the wall and another set of doors opened. The nurse led John into the connected operating room. A cart of supplies was pushed in by a second nurse while a doctor seemingly appeared from nowhere.

"Take off the jumpsuit," the nurse instructed John, "and lay on the table."

"Can I leave my underwear on?" John asked.

"Yes," the nurse nodded, "we just need access to your face and chest." John undressed and lay back on the table. He could feel the coldness of the table on his flesh as the doctor approached.

"We had to get special supplies sent from Earth," the doctor said as he was handed a needle, "if you wake up, I'll explain everything." He injected a purple-colored liquid into John's bicep.

"If?" John managed to ask before he fell unconscious.

John woke after the operation was completed. The monitor hooked to his chest alerted the doctor that John was aware. The doctor, wearing a white jumpsuit and a pleasant expression on his normal face, entered the room. John was still just dressed in his underwear but he felt different.

"How're you feeling?" The doctor asked as he pulled a chair closer to the table.

"What did you put in me?" John rubbed the spot on his arm where the needle had entered.

"Just something to knock you out," the doctor explained, "we had to cut your face open."

"My face?" John reached up and felt the skin on the right side of his face. The haggard scar was replaced by clean lines that formed a half-moon curve. His eye wasn't repaired, but his face had been slightly changed.

"What caused that scar?" The doctor asked.

"It was an accident." John answered without thinking.

"I only ask because your body had healed itself remarkably well." the doctor shrugged his shoulders.

"What do you mean?"

"Your face was partially open when you arrived. Our plan was to open your face and artificially seal it. It would've been a similar procedure done on Earth. But you," he wagged his finger, "you're something else. A shell had grown under your skin and now covers fifty percent of your skull. We just cleaned the scar lines and replaced your eye."

"What does that mean?"

"A bone-like material grew just under your skin, swallowing muscle tissue and tendons much like the Githraki skeletons that we've recovered." John thought about the accident; he remembered the pain he felt.

"What did you do to my eye?"

"That," the doctor smiled and clapped his hands, "was an achievement. Using technology usually reserved for reanimated combatants, we gave you a cyber-eye."

"Cyber-eye?" Using a complex mixture of chemicals and cyber technology, the dead were reanimated and returned to combat. Some speculated that they were superior soldiers because of their cyber enhancements while other soldiers, like John, were disgusted by them and often felt that the families of the deceased were cursed.

"It'll just take your brain a few days to get used to the implant. There may be other results, effects of the shell under your skin, which we're not aware of yet."

"I'm not human anymore."

"No," the doctor shook his head and grinned, "you're better than human."

John was allowed to redress in privacy and started to comprehend all that he'd just been told. He wanted a human eye and that was all he wanted; he never envisioned a cyber-eye. Then there was the business with his skull. He wondered if the shell had stopped growing or if it would continue; could he survive the shell's growth?

A knock came at the door as John zipped the jumpsuit closed. The time had come for him to go to the briefing. He turned and opened the door so that he could leave the medical bay, hoping that he'd never have to return.

7

"It's called Earth," General Richard Holderson said as he slowly walked through the meeting hall, "but it's far different than the world we came from.

"The environment of Jurassic Earth is deadly. This is a hostile land that will eat your soul without hesitation." He stopped at the podium in the front of the room and looked at everyone. John sat near the back, arms and legs crossed. "The Laurasia Colony is located in what will eventually be Arizona, initially colonized by the first humans to arrive in this world. There is no desert; it's a jungle." He started pacing the room. He reached into his pocket and pulled out a black rectangle. It had a clip that allowed it to be attached to the military-style jacket that Holderson wore and had ridges that reflected the lights from the ceiling. "You must follow the rules if you want to survive.

"This is an RLM," he slowed and showed the black rectangle to the assembly of soldiers and colonists, "a Radiation Level Meter. The atmosphere is thinner and the potential of skin damage from the sun is at an elevated level. Keep this pinned to your clothes at all times. Chances are that the miniature alarm in this rectangle will never go off; but there's no point in taking any chances." He reached to his belt and held up a small facemask. It was brown with straps that wound around the head. "The oxygen levels are high; so things grow big. But that also means the nitrogen levels are low. While this isn't dangerous in the short-term; humans cannot survive for extended periods of time. These masks help balance the air you breathe so that your bodies can survive it.

"But these are just gadgets in a natural world. Nature; remember that. And believe me; it *is* red in tooth and claw down there. The colony is situated in an area that many dinosaurs inhabit. Always be wary of any dinosaurs unless you positively know what you're looking at."

"Sir?" A tentative hand rose in the middle of the crowd. Holderson stopped and dropped the mask back to his belt before turning. Interruptions were frowned upon in similar meetings and Holderson didn't appear pleased. He stomped to the middle of the room with a sneer on his face.

"Identify yourself." Holderson could barely contain the spittle that threatened to spray the crowd.

"Adolph Bowers."

"Colonist or soldier?"

"Colonist." Bowers gulped.

"Good," Holderson's eyes were balls of red fury, "I wouldn't want some punk reject serving under my command." He paused. "What's your question?"

"This place might be Hell," Bowers mumbled, "but why is it just a colony?"

"Are you a mind reader, Bowers?" Holderson's voice evened out.

"No..." Bowers didn't know what else to say as his voice drifted off.

"There are plans to extend the size of the colony; the demand is present. Construction attempts have been made but they're on hold because of the Githraki," Holderson leaned against a table at the front of the hall, "for those of you unfamiliar with the alien species, I was going to elaborate.

"The Githraki are humanoids from a distant galaxy; we've been at war with them for centuries. As many of you soldiers know, the Githraki have a knack for showing-up at the worst times," John, as well as many of the other soldiers in the room, nodded, "they came to this universe through their own version of ICARUS, enslaving the humans that were already here.

"Scientists identified twelve natural dimensional holes on Earth; they open randomly and are entirely unpredictable, which was the reason ICARUS was originally built. The most infamous of these holes was the Bermuda Triangle, which happened to steal ships and planes for over a century; many soldiers may know of the disappearance of Flight 19; well, they came to this version of the planet. Since humans first appeared in the wilds of Africa they have been pulled through these dimensional holes; they have developed some technology but nothing like what we possess. They were no match for the Githraki.

"Githraki are *typically* green beings with *typically* the same number of limbs as humans. They have advanced technology and science; some would call it magic. They are highly intelligent and have enslaved humans to do their bidding. When encountered on Earth, Githraki soldiers have manipulated humans to kill our soldiers. On this world, the Githraki have enslaved humans to build their own colonies. The Githraki have control of the land around the natural dimensional holes."

"Are they dangerous?" Someone asked; John didn't see who.

"The Githraki are very dangerous but their own desire of control limits their aggressive behavior. I'd be more afraid of their human slaves. These people, which we call Amazonas, are basically the same as you and I though through evolution they've grown taller and resistant to the natural effects of this planet. They are, shall I say, primitive; but that doesn't mean they can't use the technology of their Githraki masters.

"Does that answer your question, Bowers?" Holderson looked at Adolph Bowers with a scowl. Bowers nodded but didn't dare meet Holderson's eye. "You're all registered in the colony database," Holderson continued pacing, "if you're killed by a dino, Githraki, or natural cause; an appropriate funeral will be held."

Holderson fell silent as another uniformed soldier stepped away from the wall. Holderson nodded at the soldier and turned his back to the men and women that had been listening to his talk. The other soldier raised a hand and showed everyone a manila envelope.

"You'll all be given an envelope with your particular instructions. Colonists: report to your assigned areas for deployment. You will be given more specific instructions while on the station. Soldiers: report to your assigned squad leaders for specific instructions. You're all dismissed." The room filled with muffled voices as everyone got to their feet. John waited as the crowd began shuffling out a door in the back of the room. Uniformed soldiers scanned barcodes and handed out yellow envelopes. John didn't need to open his envelope to know what was said. He just decided to keep walking, moving in the direction of the door in the front of the hall. As he approached the front of the hall, Holderson stopped him.

"You're Deacon, aren't you?" John got a good look at Holderson. Holderson was an older man with a scar crossing his throat and curled lips of disgust. He had eyes of steel that were drooped from all that they had seen. But he was strong looking; John detected no sign of fat as Holderson's suit was strained against his muscles.

"I am, sir." John nodded.

"I heard about you," Holderson pointed to John's face, "and your accident."

"How much have you heard?"

"I heard what you told your field superiors," Holderson crossed his arms in front of his chest, "but I know that you lied to them."

"Sir?" John gulped.

"Don't worry, I won't say anything."

"I just want to get this rotation done so that I can go back to active duty."

"I've served on Jurassic Earth for six rotations," Holderson said, "and I've seen things that would make you shit blue. I know that there are things in all of these universes that affect on the world we came from."

"I-"

"I've read your file," Holderson said, "I served in Afghanistan myself before your time; I know how brutal of a place it could be. Do you really want to go back there?

"I don't understand your meaning?"

"Jurassic Earth is about as close to Hell as any mortal can hope to reach," Holderson shook his head, "but it's a fresh start."

"I'm committed to my life back home."

"Do you have family or something?"

"No," John shook his head, "dead."

"It's been more than twenty years since you left; do you think that we're still at war in Afghanistan?"

"We've been fighting there for centures," John shrugged, "and we've never made any progress."

"I just want you to think about staying," Holderson whispered and pointed at John's eye again, "if you stick around I'll make sure that you get the surgery to replace your eye."

"That sounds pretty good, sir."

PART TWO
JURASSIC EARTH

8

The drop ship broke through the atmosphere as flames licked the hull. The ship's heat shield kept the passengers safe as the pilots maneuvered the bulky craft in the direction of the colony. John sat with the rest of the squad as the ship flew through the air like a giant bird of prey, eyes wide even as the turbulence shook the craft.

"Masks on," Caroline commanded the squad, "the landing strip is outside of the main colony building." The main colony building, like all of the colony buildings, had artificial air systems to make the spaces habitable without need for a breathing mask. One at a time, every member of the squad put their mask on. John looked at the other members once his own mask was on. The masks partially obscured their faces, the tinting on the glass hid most of their facial features, but they'd already been looking at each other for a few minutes.

Aside from Caroline, a young man by the name of Adrian Ball was co-squad leader. He had short hair and a stern face common among many soldiers. The two squad medics were Davis Hunt and Candy Gutierrez. They talked quietly to each other but ignored everyone else in the squad. Leonard 'Lion' Shaffer was the squad's weapon specialist and a big man that had the bruises from a brawler's life deep in the gray. Rosanna Lewis was a quiet young woman with some Hispanic ancestry; she was the one responsible for communications. Derrick McGuire was a scout, like John. He was an athlete that John recognized from television. Natalia Whitley was a thin woman with wide eyes and short hair; she was the squad's driver and had spent time in a Jurassic Earth simulation for years, training in space before leaving for the colony. Willy Hobbs was a gaunt, tall man that was the squad's demolition expert. Alyssa Patel was a sniper that had augmented her eyes to be better at killing. Elizabeth 'Liz' Benjamin was a grunt with good aim and murderous instinct.

John sat between Alyssa and Liz in silence.

"Christ, man," Liz said though her voice was slightly muffled by her mask, "what happened to your face?" There was a hiss of air following her exclamation.

"It was an accident." John replied.

"Tough shit." Liz shrugged.

"I don't care about his face," Alyssa grinned, "I'm wondering about the rest of his body." John looked at Alyssa. "I'll tell you when I'm showering," she winked, "so that you can join me." Alyssa was a thin blonde with pale skin and a heart-shaped face. She had long limbs and toned muscles.

"I'm married." John said as he turned his attention away from Alyssa.

"That's alright," her cheeks turned red in a blush, "I just want a fun way to pass the time." She'd have smiled if she could.

"You could suck my dick whenever you want," Lion leaned close to Alyssa, "I'll twist your spine and you'll enjoy every second."

"I though muscular men were compensating for what they *didn't* have between their legs." Alyssa shook her head and barked a laugh.

"What're you getting at?" Lion asked. "I'm proportionate."

"I'll believe that when I see it."

"Time and place, babe," Lion leaned back in his seat, "time and place." John smiled to himself; it was typical banter between soldiers.

"Unlike most squads, we're going to be in the main colony building," Caroline said as she pressed a blue strip against her throat. She was speaking with an advanced radio that allowed her to easily communicate with the other people in the squad. "General Holderson must have faith in us if we're going to be there."

"Why?" Willy asked with his own radio.

"Only special-op squads are housed in the main colony building," Caroline replied, "I don't know what kind of missions we'll get..." Her voice faded away as she took her hand away from her radio. She seemed momentarily lost in thought. John wondered what Caroline had done to get the squad in such a place when nobody had real experience in this world.

The ship taxied on the landing strip for a few seconds before finally coming to a halt.

"On your feet!" Adrian commanded as he walked in the direction of the doors. The other members of the squad undid their straps and rose to their feet. They formed a line behind Adrian; all of the other squads were forming lines behind their own squad leaders. The doors of the ship opened and Caroline raised her hand in a fist. "Make your way across the strip to the long building with the green roof; do not stop." The doors of the ship opened. Caroline lowered her hand and Adrian led the squad out of the ship.

Caroline was the last of the squad to leave and she took her time. With her rifle slung over her shoulder and several pistols strapped to different parts of her body, Caroline felt like a walking killing machine. By the time that she reached the building, the rest of the squad was already inside and in the process of removing their masks.

"Your eye really looks like crap." Alyssa said when she got a better look at John.

"I guess that I'm going to be doing both of our jobs." Derrick said with a smile. John was silent as he studied Derrick. His fellow scout was turning various shades of orange and red while John watched.

"Are you alright?" John asked Derrick.

"Yeah, why?"

"You're looking red and orange."

"Shit," Derrick shook his head, "you're crazy too." He turned and walked away from John as Caroline walked into the assembly and removed her own mask. As John watched, he realized that he could look through her and focus on her skeleton. Her skull was turned to him, speaking, but John didn't hear her. She moved to stand closer to him.

"Hey!" Caroline hit John in the front of the head just as John's vision was returning to normal. "Are you listening?"

"Sorry." He rubbed his eyes.

"I'm issuing formation orders so that we don't have to do this in the field."

"I'm sorry." John shook his head and tried to understand what he'd seen.

"John, I'm making you forward scout." John froze; he wasn't sure that he heard Caroline correctly. That position was reserved for the best shooter in the group; it was a title John didn't want.

"We're fucked." Derrick whispered.

"Say that again?" Caroline snapped.

"You want some unstable motherfucker going ahead of us to scope things out?" Derrick shook his head. "He'll get us all killed."

"I'm glad that you're so positive," Caroline snapped, "I hope you feel the same when you spend your days behind us."

"Scouts go in front," Derrick shook his head, "didn't you get that memo?"

"I decide who goes where," Caroline pointed her thumb at her chest, "and I've decided to put you in the rear." Caroline doled out the rest of the position assignments. Most of it was obvious; one medic would be in the center with the squad leaders in front and other guns behind. Alyssa would always remain with their vehicle while Liz would stay behind with the other medic to set up a base of operations.

Derrick was the only one that still acted like an ass. He had been upset to learn than there would be two squad leaders; he didn't want to follow anyone other than Adrian Ball.

"You're making a big mistake, ma'am." Derrick said as he shook his head. Caroline ignored him and led the way deeper into the building. The squad had entered the building near the main entrance. To the left of the entrance was the colonial government office where the governor's office was located. There were also a collection of small offices and residential cubes behind the office. At the far end of the entrance hall, opposite the doors, were stairs that led up and down. Upstairs was the research library and additional residential cubes while the downward stairs led to an enclosed outdoor training field. Caroline led the squad to the left and down a long corridor that led through the center of the building. They passed the indoor training facility and the mess hall. At the far end of the corridor were more residential cubes and the offices of the various squads. Caroline went up a set of stairs and directed the squad to a large room at the far end of the building.

Weapon racks lined one wall and a digital screen was built against the outer wall. A circular table occupied the center of the room with plenty of seats around it, digital monitors in front of each seat. It was the squad room.

"Take a seat." Caroline said. Each faux-leather chair had a name stitched in it so that everyone in the squad knew where to sit. Caroline moved to her seat at the head of the table, directly beside Adrian, as a screen on the wall perpendicular to the door was illuminated. She tapped a few keys on the digital keyboard in front of her and all of the individual monitors lit up. John found his seat and looked at his screen as Adrian spoke.

"Before we're allowed to go into the field, we all have some preparation to perform. Most of you will go to the outdoor training facility where you'll get instruction related to combat on this version of Earth. Medical team, you're headed to the med-facility to bone-up on your field medicine techniques. Rosanna, you'll need to go to the central office and learn what communication styles are used and how to operate the equipment you'll be using. Any questions?"

"I've got one," Lion raised his hand, "when do we get to shoot something?" Adrian smiled.

"Soon."

9

"Pray to whatever God you believe in," instructor Clayton McNeil said in a heavy Scottish accent as he slowly walked between the assembled soldiers and a large cage, "that you never encounter one of these bad-boys in the field." Inside the cage, heavily sedated, was a massive animal. It was almost twenty-feet long with a horn on its snout and twin ridges of bone above its large eyes. John noticed that many tranquilizer darts protruded from the animal's hide; it had taken a lot to drop it.

"What is it?" A soldier not part of Caroline's squad asked.

"This is a Ceratosaurus. It was captured when it entered the colony's perimeter a few months ago," the instructor's words were followed by hushed voices, "that's right; the colony is not always safe from dinosaurs. Many times, we see herbivorous dinosaurs near the perimeter but carnivores are sometimes drawn to us by our presence. Ceratosaurus is an ambush predator that hunts in small groups of six or seven. They are common in this area because they like hunting the sauropod herbivores that frequent the rivers around us.

"Ceratosaurus is highly intelligent, weighs up to one ton, and is powerfully built. It took ten guards and twenty tranquilizer darts to drop this single predator; imagine encountering a group of them in the wild," he laughed but the soldiers didn't find it funny, "they have excellent eyesight and thick bones that make them difficult to kill. When this one came around, the colony guards tried to kill it; but it managed to kill almost a dozen guards before tranquilizers were brought against it.

"Take note of the arms," the instructor turned his body and indicated the sprawled arms protruding from under the dinosaur, "the arms are relatively short for a carnivore of this size but it has four fingers which make the hands useful. Notice the horn and bone ridges on the skull; those are not weapons but getting struck with one will still hurt." McNeil paused. "Never engage one of these animals if you can avoid it; they are aggressive and they will kill you. The weapons that you'll be carrying can be effective if you can get a decent shot in; but that's highly unlikely." He started walking and the soldiers followed.

McNeil stopped in front of another cage, though much larger than the Ceratosaurus's cell and the residents were fully conscious. There were two animals inside, both enormous with long necks and grey skin. They had the dumb look of domesticated pets. McNeil pointed at the two animals which were chewing grass while eyeing the drugged Ceratosaurus.

"Ceratosaurus is fond of hunting these dinosaurs," the instructor explained, "They are both Camarasaurs. The Ceratosaurus followed these two, and their herd, into our perimeter though the adults Camarasaurs escaped. These two are juveniles, roughly fifty feet from snout to the tip of the tail. These guys are males; adult males are likely to bully each other. They are herbivorous and must consume large amounts of plant material each day to sustain their massive bodies. You should see their shit." He laughed again and wiped a humorous tear from his face. "They're relatively stupid, as most sauropods are, but their size makes them formidable against carnivores like Ceratosaurus. These guys each weigh about 18 tons. But what you might find surprising is that Camarasaurus is one of the smallest sauropods in the region.

"Now, I'm sure that some of you are excited about the last dinosaur we've caught." McNeil smiled and waved so that the soldiers followed, "this guy was found outside of the perimeter. He was injured from a nasty fall and would've died had we not intervened. I present: Stegosaurus." The Stegosaurus was eating a fern and drinking from an artificial pond when the soldiers approached. It turned its small head and looked at them but made no additional movement other than to slightly swing its tail. It was a bulky dinosaur, almost half as long as the Camarasaurs, with short front legs and powerful back legs. Small, boney protrusions rose from its shoulders. Twin rows of red plates rose from its neck, following the curve of its spine, and terminated at the tail. The tail was a weapon: eight angled spikes, each about four feet long, pointed to the sides of the tail like a medieval mace.

"Is it dangerous?" Caroline asked nervously.

"Yes," McNeil nodded, "although it's an herbivore, Stegosaurs are temperamental and can kill if threatened. They don't typically form herds, though juveniles are sometimes seen with adults. This particular Stegosaurus is an *ugulatis*, identifiable by the number of tail spikes. Typical Stegosaurs just have four spikes." McNeil was interrupted by a resounding roar that came from the Ceratosaurus cage. McNeil frowned. "Shit," he muttered, "the Ceratosaurus is awake. I told them that they needed to inject high doses of tranquilizers into him."

McNeil jogged back to the Ceratosaur cage while numerous armed guards ran across the training field. The soldiers watched, fascinated. Caroline walked up to John and whispered in his ear.

"Keep and eye on them," she said, "you'll probably notice one of these guys before the rest of us." She took a step back and John nodded. The Camarasaurs looked at the Ceratosaurus with mild interest while the Stegosaurus was completely uninterested. John suspected that the tail spikes were effective against most carnivores.

The guards all carried high-capacity rifles that were loaded with tranquilizer darts. Dressed in black clothing and polished boots, the guards took up position around the Ceratosaurus. They took aim at the Ceratosaur's flank as it slowly moved in circles inside the cage. McNeil had his face set as he watched the irritated carnivore.

"Fire at will." He said. The command was repeated by a guard standing beside McNeil. The guards began firing darts at the Ceratosaurus until its legs buckled and it fell back to its belly. McNeil shook his head as the guards moved away. The instructor returned to the soldiers and looked at each of them.

"Why were you so concerned about it?" John asked.

"Ceratosaurs are highly intelligent," McNeil said with his head bowed, "they respond to the distress calls of other Ceratosaurs. Worse than that, other carnivores can be attracted."

"What kind of carnivores?" A soldier asked.

"The worst in the region," McNeil frowned, "Allosaurus."

10

The training dummy was fifty yards away but John raised his rifle. He was in an enclosed box with bulletproof walls that prevented him from either seeing or shooting his fellow soldiers. His only option was to shoot the dummy.

As he concentrated, John became aware that his vision was changing. At first he could just see the dummy; but his new vision allowed him to see the gravity pull, artificial wind, and the "invisible" lasers that were intended to destroy his bullet. The idea was to simulate the difficulties present in Jurassic Earth.

While he'd originally aimed straight, John's new vision showed that the combined gravity pull and artificial wind would push his bullet into a laser. But a higher shot...

John adjusted his aim and squeezed the trigger. The bullet arced through the air at high speed, just grazing one of the horizontal lasers. The laser, rather that turn his bullet to dust, put additional spin on the bullet as the combined effects of gravity and air altered the bullet's trajectory.

The bullet struck the dummy in the chest and burned a hole to the wall behind it. A small screen beside John's head clicked on and the face of the training coach appeared.

"Good shot, Deacon," the training coach said with an electronic tinge to his voice, "nobody has ever hit the dummy in the chest on their first attempt. I'll chalk it up to luck; but if you can do it again, I'll buy your rations for a week." The face disappeared and John watched as the damaged dummy was automatically replaced with a new dummy.

John concentrated again. He noticed that the lasers pointed in new directions as the artificial wind was altered. The coach was trying to confuse him. John smiled as he lowered his aim. He squeezed the trigger.

The bullet went above one laser and below another as it ricocheted off the floor. Propelled by sheer force, without wind to change its course, the bullet struck the dummy in the chest. John put the rifle on the flat surface in front of him and smiled.

The screen clicked on again.

"Shit." The coach muttered. John was aware how expensive rations were and he knew that the coach was regretting his offer.

"I think that you owe me a week's worth of food." John smiled.

"Alright," the coach nodded, "but I've got something I want you to try." The door behind John clicked open and a black-clad guard carried a strange rifle that John couldn't identify. The guard took John's practice rifle and the door closed. John looked at the screen.

"What's this?" John held up the weapon.

"High-capacity multi-purpose rifle," the coach said, "it holds less ammunition but packs a stronger punch."

"Why aren't these weapons standard issue?"

"The cost of a single high-capacity multi-purpose rifle is the equivalent of one-thousand standard rifles," the coach explained, "before the additional cost of shipping them here. This is not a practice weapon; this is the rifle that you'll carry into combat."

"I've never heard of this gun before." John inspected it. It was sleek with curved edges, a reformatted stock to absorb recoil, grenade launcher, laser scope, auto-targeting computer, and special attachments that John didn't recognize.

"I'm not surprised," the coach shrugged, "this rifle was reverse-engineered from found Githraki technology."

"Alien technology." John muttered to himself. He raised the rifle and closed his left eye. What he saw shocked him; he was looking *through* the rifle scope without putting it to his face. He lowered the rifle to his waist and his vision returned to normal.

"Take care of her," the coach said, "you won't get another."

"I'll remember that."

"This is the MKII, the battle-armor you'll all wear when outside of the compound," a woman hissed as she paced the large room, "it, and its components, are essential to your survival." The MKII behind her was in the shape of a man, completely obscuring the dummy beneath. It was dull gray with a tinted facemask and full articulation on all limbs and neck. The "skin" was covered with a metal composite that was fully articulated and jointed to allow for movement. The chest and stomach appeared connected but they were really two separate plates that locked like the shell of a beetle. The few points of the body that couldn't be covered by armor, like the backs of the knees and the inside of the elbows, were covered by a black mesh that John recognized. "This is a variant of the battle-armor that most of you soldiers have used before; the MKI suits.

"The MKI suits are designed for the environment that they're going to be in while the MKII can be deployed in every environment. Many soldier here served in desert and urban warfare: MKI suits in those places were equipped with personal air conditioners and spotlights, and they're colored to be representative of the environment. The MKII suits have all the amenities possible to those suits, including the helmets that allow you to survive and computer display screens so that you can communicate with the colony computer whenever you need too.

"I won't lie, these suits have limitations. For example, the helms entirely obscure your faces and make it impossible to speak or hear; so each helm is equipped with radios so that they can communicate with each other and anyone not in armor.

"Now-"

"There are weaknesses." John mumbled; but in the silence, everyone could hear him.

"Excuse me?" The instructor stopped and looked right at John, keeping a calm but otherwise emotionless expression on her face.

"I said that there are weaknesses that you haven't mentioned." John clarified.

"I was going to get to them," she cleared her throat, "these suits are machines and subject to the damages machines are weak against. They can be dented; many dinosaurs in the region are strong enough to inflict serious amounts of physical damage. Since there is a lot of metal, the suits can rust and fall apart. If that happens, remember that Jurassic air will enter the suit and you won't be able to breath. Then there are the servos.

"There are servos all over the suit. They assist with movement, management, and operation. Most of the servos are secured under armor but can be triggered by damage done to the suit."

"There are weapons that you must be familiar with other that your primary armament," the weapons instructor stood in front of a metal table and spoke to a small group of soldiers. John paid attention, his arms folded close against his chest, "this is a standard handgun with standard rounds; most of you have used this type of weapon before." The instructor held up a black gun with a short barrel and wide trigger to make it easy to hold in armor. He put the gun down and showed everyone a serrated knife. "This knife has a blade roughly sixteen inches long, serrated on one side, and is molded out of Githraki carbon with a hollow core. The core is filled with liquid metal. It looks like a typical knife, evenly weighted, but it is strong enough to cut through most things."

11

The rotors started to spin as the control board lit up. Natalia was strapped in with shoulder harnesses but that didn't stop her from slipping a cigarette into her mouth; she wasn't going to smoke but wanted the taste of the nicotine. Her light helmet kept her blonde hair from getting in her face and the goggles that she wore allowed her to see through adverse weather conditions.

The staff, which looked like a black stick, was positioned between her thighs. Alone in the cockpit, in a space reminiscent of a coffin, she communicated with the rest of the squad via a communicator strapped to her throat.

"Ready to fly?" She asked. The rotors were spinning so fast that they were hardly visible as the horizontal wings began to move so that the rotors were pointed at the sky. The cockpit closed and locked shut so that Natalia would be able to breathe without the use of a mask. The rest of the squad waited patiently in the Raptor's rear hold while Alyssa and Liz, both in full battle armor, took positions at the guns that flanked the rear hold and looked out over the jungle.

Natalia wondered who named the aerial vehicles 'Raptors,' if it had happened in their time as a joke or if it had been someone on Jurassic Earth. Either way, the name was both ominous and hilarious. At the very least they wouldn't encounter any raptors.

The doors above the hangar opened and the Raptor lifted into the sky. Once it had reached a safe altitude, the rotors spun forward again and the Raptor moved through the skies. Natalia barely had to touch the staff to change directions, a difference between aircraft that she'd flown in the military and the Jurassic Earth variety. She also knew that the sensitivity was essential; they weren't the only creatures in the sky.

"One mile west we'll reach a river," Caroline was reading a map while communicating with Natalia, "at that point, turn north until we reach a beach. Then, land on the beach and set-up base camp there." Caroline and the rest of the squad didn't need communicators like Natalia since their helmets provided everything that they could need.

"Roger," Natalia replied, "who's idea was it to go this way?"

"There's an Amazonas settlement near the beach reinforced with Githraki weaponry," Caroline repeated the instructions that she'd been given, "we're tasked with observation."

"Why?"

"We're not paid to ask why." Caroline snapped. The rest of the squad turned to look at her but said nothing.

"I'm just wondering why we're using a river as a landmark." Natalia's voice said dryly.

"As we approach any Githraki settlement, including Amazonas settlements, instrumentation tends to fail; we don't know why." Caroline shrugged but her movement went unnoticed.

"I was studying local dinosaurs," Natalia said, "and the studies showed that many carnivorous dinosaurs hunt near rivers."

"We'll be fine." Caroline didn't really believe her own words.

"I don't want to be a bother," Natalia's voice dropped to almost a whisper, "but if we're forced to drop because of an aerial predator..." Natalia didn't finish the thought.

"What?" Alyssa asked though she kept her focus on the skies around the Raptor.

"An Allosaurus could snatch us out of the sky." Natalia said. The squad didn't respond; they all knew the dangers posed by Allosaurs.

Natalia moved the Raptor forward, heading in the instructed directions, as the thick Jurassic jungle spread out beneath them. Liz tapped the binocular controls on the side of her helmet as she observed the surrounding area.

"There's a volcano due west." Liz said.

"There is a massive Githraki settlement located near that volcano," Adrian said with closed eyes, "our scans can show us that much."

"Should the Amazonas be considered a threat?" Derrick asked.

"Let's just say," Adrian paused, "that they don't like us." He laughed softly but the other members of the squad ignored his version of humor.

As the Raptor moved over the jungle, Alyssa noticed movement on the ground. She activated her own binocular vision with the push of a button on the side of her helmet and clearly watched armed soldiers moving slowly while a black machine lumbered behind them like a black lizard.

"What is that?" Alyssa asked as her helmet vision returned to normal. Caroline carefully moved beside Alyssa, holding onto a safety strap for support, and looked down to the jungle.

"That is an iguana-tron." Caroline said.

"An iguana-tron is a single-person machine covered in various weaponry," Natalia added through the radio, "I've never piloted one, just simulation."

"Where're they going?" Alyssa asked.

"Probably toward the Amazonas," Caroline said, "the iguana-tron moves slowly and the jungle doesn't make moving any easier. It'll take them some time to get there."

"What about the river?" Alyssa asked.

"The iguana-tron will have to find another way across." Caroline said.

"Oh." Alyssa shook her head. She wondered what the colony leaders were doing.

The Raptor moved through low clouds as it approached the river. A red light flashed on the dash, accompanied by a monotonous *beep* sound. Natalia looked at the dials and display screen; she was notified by computer that there was an aerial animal flying above the river.

"Anyone see it?" Natalia tapped her communicator. Liz responded.

"I've spotted it," Liz said softly, "it's huge." 'Huge' was an understatement; it was bigger than the Raptor. It had a wingspan that stretched over thirty-feet with a thin body that was hardly visible between the two wings, light fur on its whole body, a brightly colored crest above its small eyes and a beak that put its wings to shame. Liz trained her gun on it but didn't fire.

"Maybe it'll leave us alone," Caroline sounded hopeful, "Natalia; swing north but keep the river in sight. We'll continue on our scheduled course."

"Copy." Natalia's response came as the Raptor arced into a turn and headed north. Everyone was feeling better until the aerial predator shifted its body to intercept the Raptor. Natalia watched, fascinated, from the safety of the cockpit. "That is a beautiful aerial creature." Her eyes widened.

"Is it going to attack?" Derrick asked.

"Hold on," Natalia removed one hand from the staff and touched a series of buttons on the computer console, "computer: identify the dinosaur." She commanded the computer once a white screen illuminated on the dash.

"*There are no dinosaurs in range.*"

"Then what is that thing in the sky?"

"*Dinosaurs are strictly land-based animals. The aerial animal is a Quetzalcoatlus. It is rare during this period of time as other Pterasaurs are common; Quetzalcoatlus remains have only ever been discovered in conjunction with Late-Cretaceous formations. However, since the animal's body is light and hollow, it is possible that they lived earlier than discovered by paleontologists.*

"*The maximum wingspan for Quetzalcoatlus is just less than thirty-six feet. No flying animal is known to be larger. Its weight is roughly three-hundred pounds, despite its size. Both the head and legs exceed seven feet in length. It is highly intelligent with a large brain and binocular vision to assist it hunting. The crest is primarily a sexual display, only males have colored crests.*

"*The wings are made of a leather-like membrane that is more than nine inches thick where the wings connect to the torso. The wings connect the fourth, elongated finger to the upper torso and legs. Quetzalcoatlus has only a rudimentary tail and must rely on updrafts for flight – it is too large to flap its wings.*

"*Quetzalcoatlus is a carnivore but feeds mainly on fish and small animals living near rivers. Humans are too large to be considered viable food unless they are severely injured and pose no threat to the animal. Quetzalcoatlus is not a threat unless a male is confronted during mating season. Males, during this period, can be identified by brightly colored crests and heads. During mating season, males will attack other aerial objects to defend their large territory, allowing only female Quetzalcoatlus to approach.*"

"Is the one flying at us preparing to mate?" Natalia asked the computer.

"*Negative; Quetzalcoatlus mating grounds are primarily in Mexico and nearby areas, in accordance with research. This is a young male that is not fully prepared for the flight.*

"*Additionally, Quetzalcoatlus mating season is in the summer.*" The computer sounded as though it were mocking her.

"Fine," Natalia muttered as the computer clicked off and she tapped the communicator on her thoat, "everybody hang-on!" She nosed the Raptor down and clenched her teeth. The Raptor dipped forward and dove at the jungle, forcing the Quetzalcoatlus to follow. The animal dove, angling its wings to move faster.

"This guy won't give-up." Liz cursed as she pulled the trigger on her rifle. Bullets flew at the Quetzalcoatlus but the animal dodged the barrage by continually shifting its body. One bullet struck the crest but was deflected by the thick bone. The Quetzalcoatlus screamed to reveal a toothless maw.

The Raptor moved in a complex spin that increased its speed, all the passengers had to grab hold of something or else they risked being thrown from the craft. The Quetzalcoatlus spread its wings wide and let the heat from the jungle provide lift. It rose away from the Raptor as the vehicle continued to dive.

"I think we're safe," Caroline radioed Natalia as she struggled to hold on to a bar near the port door but no response came as the Raptor continued its plunge, "Natalia?"

"I can't regain control," her voice sounded strained, "I can only make the crash less-severe!"

"Crash?" Alyssa turned her head as far as her armor allowed.

"Everybody out!" Caroline yelled. The squad leapt from Raptor as HALO parachutes opened from their backs; the gunners released the straps holding them to their seats and pushed away, their arms spread like birds. Natalia's cockpit blasted open with the use of small explosives and flew above the falling Raptor. Natalia inhaled and held her breath as she reached for her helmet and put it on, sliding the rubber neck around her throat until the metal clamp clicked shut. She didn't dare breathe the Jurassic air even as her eyes started to burn. She clicked the helm to the rest of her suit, hearing a reassuring *hiss*, seconds before her seat was launched into the sky.

Natalia could breathe again as the Raptor erupted into flames beneath her. She let out a sigh and looked at the wreckage. What she saw upset her: the flames were rising into the sky at her as the wings crumpled like paper on nearby rocks and the numerous trees. Moments later, the flames caught Natalia's parachute and turned it to ash.

"No!" Natalia screamed but her radio, momentarily unplugged as wreckage from the Raptor flew around her, forced her scream into the nothingness of silence.

Natalia fell to the ground, losing consciousness just before she struck the highest branches of the trees.

12

John pulled himself away from his parachute, using his knife to cut the nylon cords, as he moved for cover near a small rock outcropping. He looked up to the sky as Natalia's frail body fell to the trees. He lost sight of her in the canopy.

"Natalia?" He cursed and ran from his hiding spot toward the place Natalia should've landed. He jumped through oppressive ferns and rolled under broken logs until he came to a small clearing, the gears in the armor *whirred* as he rolled. John stopped and looked around until a voice in his head told him to look up. He tilted his head and froze; Natalia's ropes were snagged on the canopy fifty-feet above the ground. She was unconscious, her body limp.

"Damn..." Caroline jogged into the clearing and saw Natalia. Her rifle, which she'd carried as though she was rushing into battle, dropped to her side. Adrian appeared next and was similarly shocked by what he saw. Candy, a fit woman in her twenties with thin hips and long legs, dashed into the clearing while Davis, shorter and bulkier, carried the medical supplies on his back. Candy was supposed to stay with the Raptor to help set-up base camp though that seemed silly at the moment.

"Is she dead?" John asked.

"I don't detect any movement," Candy looked at Natalia and then turned to Davis, "what about you?" Davis dropped the packs he'd been carrying and tapped the bio-scanner on his helmet. He looked at Natalia and tried to detect her vital signs but she was too far away for a decent analysis.

"*Scanning...*" There was a moment of silence. "*Unable to detect Whitley, Natalia.*"

"The computer can't detect life," Davis said with a resigned sigh, "and I don't see anything." He was disappointed; he'd watched Natalia walking with an interest in her butt.

"We can't leave her up there," Caroline said, "A predator would find us." John glanced at Caroline; she was thinking like a squad leader but not like a human. John looked away, disappointed.

"Better her than us," Adrian turned to look at Caroline, "she's already dead." John continued to watch and focused on Natalia. He didn't know what was happening, but he sensed her heartbeat.

Her heart was working and Natalia was breathing.

"She's alive." John whispered.

"How do you know that?" Candy asked, looking at John with narrow eyes. She knew that John had been given a cyber-eye before passing through ICARUS but she didn't know everything; she didn't know about the alien shell courtesy of the Githraki.

"She's alive," John turned to look at the skeptical medic, "trust me." Derrick stepped into the clearing, his steps unsteady.

"How do you propose that we get her down?" Adrian asked. "Are you going to climb up there?" Alyssa and Liz strolled into the clearing together. Liz was watching the surrounding area while Alyssa went through the process of reconfiguring her rifle. As the squad's sniper, Alyssa was the only person to carry a sniper-combat rifle.

"I think that you're all thinking too much." Alyssa said. John detected a change in her speaking and looked at Alyssa. Nobody knew about the damage she'd taken when she fell through the trees.

"What do you mean?" Caroline asked.

"John and Derrick, position yourselves beneath Natalia," Alyssa instructed the scouts as she raised her sniper rifle at Natalia, "catch her before she hits the ground."

"What?" Derrick asked but Alyssa had already pulled the trigger. Her shot destroyed a nearly invisible nylon cord that was wrapped around a branch. Natalia fell faster than anyone expected.

Derrick still moved slowly as John ran under Natalia. Even as he moved, John knew that his position was wrong. As he'd detected the bullet trajectory during training, he knew that the angle of Natalia's fall would be different than expected. He moved a yard further than anyone would've anticipated and bent his legs.

Natalia fell and John caught her. His legs bent a little but John felt additional strength in his body to support Natalia. He shifted his body and lowered her to the ground. Candy and Davis rushed over, Davis still lugging the medical supplies.

"Computer: report vitals." Candy commanded. The small computers that everyone in the squad wore allowed her to communicate directly with Natalia's computer.

"*Scanning... Breathing: optimal. Airway: slightly obstructed. Pulse: steady.*"

"Computer: increase airflow until the airway loosens; then inject steroids to prevent the throat from closing." Candy said as she and Davis took positions on either side of Natalia. Natalia's pressure-suit hummed as the motors increased the airflow against Natalia's face.

"Computer: report on spinal injury." Davis commanded.

"*Bruising discovered; no severe spinal injury detected.*" Davis turned his head to Candy but their helmets prevented him from looking in her eyes.

"Turn her?" Davis asked Candy.

"Turn her." Candy agreed. Davis helped turned Natalia on her side so that she was facing Candy. While Davis started to lift Natalia's upper leg into a right-angle position against her hip, Candy slowly tilted Natalia's head back to prevent damage to her airway.

"Computer: increase heat pressure by one degree." Candy said. The computer complied and there was a beep as the temperature rose. The beep would've triggered an alarm if anyone that wasn't a registered medic issued the command.

"Can you hear me?" Candy asked as she lowered her head to be close to Natalia's face. Natalia moaned.

"Is she alright?" Caroline asked but Candy didn't respond.

"What is your name?" Candy asked Natalia.

"Natalie Isabella Whitley." Natalia answered. She used the name given by her parents, not the slight change that she adopted when she became an adult.

"When were you born?"

"Christmas." Candy thought that she detected a smile but there was no way to check.

"How old are you?"

"Fifty-one." Natalia said with a small laugh.

"How old were you when you left Earth?" John asked, interrupting Candy.

"Twenty-seven."

"She'll be alright," Candy reported to the squad, "though we should let her rest before moving her far."

"We'll set-up camp here," Caroline said as she looked around, "John, Derrick, Lion; I want you three to form a perimeter while we prepare camp. You'll be relieved as necessary."

"That sounds good to me." Lion said.

"I don't like staying in this clearing," Derrick shook his head, "there's no natural protection."

"You heard Candy," Caroline said, "we need to keep Natalia here while she rests."

"Stop..." John was about to speak when he was overcome by a sense of fear. "Something is coming."

"What is it?" Derrick asked. He was standing near the tree-line, rifle at his side, looking at John. He was entirely relaxed. He didn't suspect anything.

That was when the large, tooth-filled head burst out of the shadows and bit into Derrick. He was ripped in half by the dinosaur's sharp teeth as it pulled him into the trees; there was a brief scream that was immediately followed by silence. The dinosaur was larger than the Ceratosaurus but appeared more lethal. It had a long head with narrow eyes; it was striped like a tiger of old though colored brown and yellow.

There was a deafening roar as another dinosaur stepped out of the trees, fully revealing its massive bulk; it was basically a therapod with muscular legs and flexible arms, though it appeared to limp a little from an old wound in its right foot. It had serrated teeth that had evidence of decaying flesh lingering. It had three-fingered hands, each digit equipped with an evil claw that worked continually as though they were highly maneuverable. Its eyes looked at each squad member individually; John suspected that it was highly intelligent. It had rough, pebbly skin and some of the bones, all thick and powerful, were visible. The dinosaur moved cautiously, each step covering four feet easily. It had a thick tail that was kept at a 90 degree angle against its hips.

John had the sensation that a third was circling the clearing to attack from the rear.

"We should go." Adrian whispered quietly as he began to step away from the dinosaur threat without looking around.

"There's another one behind us," John spoke in a quiet voice, "let's go a different way." Adrian froze.

"Everyone to the eastern edge of the clearing," Caroline quietly ordered, "now!"

"Help me move her." Candy said to Davis. The two medics carefully lifted Natalia off the ground and carried her after the rest of the squad. The dinosaur that had fully revealed itself lunged forward and landed where Natalia had been. Any hope for a fatal fall was forgotten as the dinosaur carefully rose to its feet; it wobbled a little but didn't appear that it was bothered by the injury to its foot.

John slowed and stopped, turning back to the clearing and aimed with his rifle. The injured dinosaur was his best target.

"I hope the rest like fresh meat." John said as he pulled the trigger. Three bullets flashed from the muzzle like balls of light just before striking the limping dinosaur in the head. The dinosaur fell back to the ground, everything above the s-shaped neck gone. The other dinosaurs paused as they considered pursuing the fleeing humans but the prospect of an easy meal dissuaded them.

The squad was able to run without fear of pursuit.

13

A small camp was set up at one side of a rocky ravine but no fire was lit. Small dinosaurs that were roughly the size of chickens scurried around but none approached the camp or the dangerous humans. John and Lion had taken posts a short distance from the camp; if any curious dinosaur approached, they'd be ready.

"What was that thing?" Adrian asked as Candy and Davis continued monitoring Natalia's vitals.

"Computer; can you identify?" Caroline asked.

"*Negative. HQ is out of range; DECEASED report will be sent to Colony HQ once in range.*" The computer responded.

"We're stuck out here until help arrives." Alyssa muttered. She leaned against a moldy rock and cradled her rifle, eyes closed.

"No," Caroline sighed, "help won't be sent." Adrian turned his head toward her. She looked at Adrian.

"What?" Liz asked, sitting up.

"Help won't be sent from the colony," Caroline explained, "it's against protocol."

"Fuck protocol," Adrian cursed, "we won't survive out here for long." Adrian shook his head and looked away.

"Can we walk back?" Alyssa asked.

"Too... far." Natalia muttered. Candy and Davis checked on her but they were both confident that Natalia was recovering quickly.

"We'll have to wait for the Iguana-tron," Caroline said, "but we don't know if it'll even come this way."

"What do we do?" Liz asked. She was both communicating with Caroline and monitoring the edge of the ravine.

"The Amazonas are close," Rosanna shrugged, "we can walk that distance in a few hours." She shook her head. "Hell, they might already know that we're here."

"Yeah," Adrian laughed, "because *that* is a good plan."

"Any plan is a good plan." Caroline said.

"I'd rather walk home."

"It's our best chance to survive," Caroline said, "that's final."

"I'm not going."

"Do you want to die out here?"

"Here or there; both seem likely."

Caroline knew that Adrian was stubborn.

"Listen-up," all of the squad members could hear Caroline when she tapped on the radio attached to her throat, "the plan is to leave for the nearby Amazonas camp in the morning. Adrian does not want to go and would rather attempt to return to the colony. Is anyone willing to go with him?"

"I'll go." Lion replied instantly.

"One of us should go," Davis said, "just incase something happens." He spoke directly to Candy.

"Who?" Candy asked.

"Let fate decide," Davis held up his hand in a fist. He wanted to play rock-paper-scissors, "the winner goes to the colony."

"You've got to be joking."

"One-two-three..." Davis jerked his hand. Candy quickly made a fist.

"Shoot!" Candy said. Both medics made either a fist for a rock, a flat hand for paper, or two fingers for scissors. Candy kept her hand as a fist while Davis flattened his hand.

"Paper beats Rock," he said to Candy before turning his head to Caroline, "I'm going back to the colony."

"I'll go," Liz said, "they'll need a good gun." There was no arguing the point.

"Natalia will have to go with us," Candy said, "she can't survive going back to the colony."

"Alright." Caroline shook her head.

"We split up in the morning." Adrian said. Caroline looked at Adrian. Neither expected the other to survive; neither was entirely sure that their plan was best.

"Good luck." Caroline whispered to Adrian.

"I hope that we both make it back." Adrian said.

"If we do," Caroline said, "make sure that they serve steak in the mess."

"That goes for both of us."

Willy struggled to support Natalia as helped carry her out of the ravine and deeper into the jungle. Candy, who was about the same height as Natalia, had little problem. But Willy was much shorter; he kept quite and didn't alert Candy to his trouble until it was too late.

"Am I going to carry her by myself?" Candy cursed.

"I've got it." Willy grumbled. Candy shook her head but remained focused on Caroline. The squad had just divided and it was hard; neither group knew who was going to succeed but both hoped that the entire squad would eventually reach the colony.

"I can walk," Natalia muttered, "just let me try."

"You can try," Candy grimaced, "when we reach level ground. It's too rocky here; your injury would be serious if you fell." She didn't want to admit that she was mostly responsible for carrying Natalia since Willy wasn't doing much work on his own.

"Quiet," Caroline put a finger to her helm, "those dinosaurs could be close." She hoped that she was wrong but she couldn't be sure. Caroline and Rosanna walked a few yards in front of Candy, Natalia, and Willy; John was forward of them and Alyssa brought up the rear.

"Caroline," John's voice was soft as it came through the comm. system, "you're not going to believe this."

"What?" Caroline stopped walking.

"Trust me," Caroline detected a smile, "you'll want to see this."

Adrian pushed his group hard; it was a long trek back to the colony. He wanted to be back in a few days, no more. As strong as he was, the same couldn't be said for the other members of the group. Davis was huffing and puffing as he struggled to keep up.

"Come-on," Adrian urged Davis to continue, "you've almost made it." They'd been climbing a hill that was almost at forty-five degrees, testing everyone's reserve. It took several agonizing minutes but the group eventually crested the hill. The descent was much faster but nobody cared.

A carnivorous dinosaur was sleeping a few yards away, the flies from its latest kill buzzing around its tooth-filled maw. It was larger than the dinosaurs that had attacked in the clearing, but this was a solitary predator. Its arms, which were partially hidden by its bulk, were long and each finger had a hooked claw on it. Its teeth were sickle shaped and clearly visible, despite the flies.

"Everyone be quiet." Adrian commanded. Since he communicated through the helmet system, he didn't alert the dinosaur to their presence.

"I hope it ate something big," Liz whispered, "I'd hate to see this thing coming after us." She took a step forward and broke a branch in half. The *snap* sounded like a gunshot in the silence. The dinosaur lazily pushed itself up and rose to its feet. It was a massive killer with large nostrils and intelligent eyes. It yawned and turned its head at the group of humans.

It roared.

The humans backpedaled and tried to move down the hill, but the dinosaur was faster. It covered the few yards in seconds and knocked Adrian off of his feet. The squad commander tumbled to the side of the clearing, momentarily dazed. Davis, unable to run, was kicked back just before the dinosaur's clawed feet sank into his chest; sparks from his MKII suit erupted as blood stained the ground. He screamed once before he was enveloped by darkness. Lion raised his rifle and shot at the dinosaur, but all he managed to do was strike bone. The dinosaur hardly gave him a moment's thought as it bit down on Davis' corpse and swung its tail at Lion, striking the man with enough force to break bone. The suit held him together but Lion wasn't strong enough to survive the assault.

Lion's ribcage broke and he suffocated, forced to swallow the blood that he coughed up from his broken lungs.

Liz half ran and half rolled down the hill in her escape attempt, her suit continuously moving. She hit rocks and trees but remained conscious. She knew that the dinosaur wasn't following her; she also knew that Adrian was still alive. She climbed to her feet in an attempt to save him; but, fear stopped her and she turned away in hopes of catching up with the rest of the squad.

Adrian tried to crawl to safety inside a log while the dinosaur savagely tore at Davis' body. He didn't dare look back; all he wanted was to survive. There wasn't a lot of room for the large dinosaur to maneuver; he hoped that the cover would be enough. At last he reached cover; he was sure that the rest of the squad was dead as he heard the dinosaur roar again.

He took several deep breathes before he fell asleep; exhausted.

14

The trees thinned at the edge of a valley. John had his rifle shouldered as the rest of the squad approached. They were apprehensive until they saw the sight before them. They were on a slight rise, the dinosaurs below them. Everyone's guard dropped as a gentle breeze blew toward them.

"Beauty is a manifestation of secret natural laws, which otherwise would have been hidden from us forever." Caroline whispered under her breath.

"Who said that?" Natalia asked.

"Johann Wolfgang von Goethe," Caroline turned to look at Natalia, "I went to college before joining the army." Few people knew that, fewer people cared. 'Beauty' was the best word to describe the sight at the bottom of the rise.

A herd of large, gray animals slowly moved through an open space with a herd of relatively smaller animals following. The smaller animals weren't that small, but they were tiny compared to the larger animals.

"Computer," Caroline said quietly as though her voice would decimate the scene, "can you identify these animals?"

"*Specify.*" The computer's response was immediate.

"The big ones."

"*Specify.*"

"Specify? Do I need to draw you a picture? The bigger fuckin' dinosaurs!" Caroline snapped.

"*Diplodocus is one of the largest land animals that ever lived. It has a long neck that is counterbalanced by an equally long, whip-like tail. The average size of an adult Diplodocus is ninety-feet, though they can be as short as seventy-five feet or as long as one-hundred and ten feet. It is herbivorous.*

"*Diplodocus is lighter than other giant sauropods, weighing between ten and twenty tons. The spine is made of strong vertebrae that support its massive bulk; and also provide the small spikes that cover its torso. The tail can be used as a weapon against predators; the tail has spikes running along its length. But because of its size, few predators would risk encountering a Diplodocus.*

"*Diplodocus is not very intelligent. Like all sauropods, it relies on instinct more than thought. Because of this, they often travel with other herbivorous dinosaurs.*"

"Can you identify the other dinosaurs?"

"*Camptosaurus is a herbivorous dinosaur that measures between sixteen and twenty-three feet long. It is primarily green with stripes of white and yellow that offer it a measure of camouflage. Despite its bulk of over two-thousand pounds, Camptosaurus can run if necessary. Typical locomotion involves walking on four legs, especially when in the company of sauropods.*"

"*Camptosaurus is slightly intelligent; more so than sauropods but less intelligent than most carnivores.*"

"*Camptosaurus has a beak which is used to chew low vegetation; however, it will eat plant matter dropped by sauropods.*" That was what the Camptosaurs were doing; eating vegetation dropped by the Diplodocus that they walked beside. The squad noticed that there were no young Diplodocus around, but infant Camptosaurs played in the center of the herd.

"I wonder where the babies are." Alyssa remarked.

"Leave those questions for the paleontologists," Caroline shrugged, "we've got to keep moving."

"Wait," John held up his hand, "someone is coming." He turned and aimed his rifle at a nearby bush when Liz burst through. Her armor was covered in dirt and muck and her skin, hidden beneath the armor, was soaked in sweat.

"Liz?" Caroline took a step forward. "What happened?"

"We... we were attacked," Liz explained, "everyone else is dead." She fought to catch her breath. The regulator in her suit clicked on to aid her.

"What happened to you?"

"I rolled down a hill," Liz shook her head, "and then I stumbled through a small bog. I was hoping to find you all before you went far."

"You found us." Candy said.

"Yeah," Liz swallowed, "thank God for that." Natalia was walking by herself without problem as the squad moved out of the trees and into the field. The dinosaurs watched but none seemed offended by the presence of humans. If anything, they were indifferent. Liz was thankful for that; she had her fill.

"Computer; detect damaged bones." Candy said. The computer whirred for a second before it responded.

"I told you that I'm fine." Liz said to Candy.

"You might feel fine," Candy said, "but you could still have broken or damaged bones."

"*Benjamin, Elizabeth: satisfactory.*" The computer said to Candy. Liz felt better about herself.

"Are you satisfied?"

"Not really." Candy frowned.

"Computer," Caroline was walking a few yards away but lost in thought, "detect squad vitals."

"*Scanning...*" There was a moment of silence as the computer searched for nearby computers. "*West, Caroline: Vital signs nominal. Gutierrez, Rachel: Vital signs nominal. Lewis, Rosanna: Vital signs nominal. Deacon, John: Vital signs nominal as previously documented. Whitley, Natalia: Vital signs nominal. Hobbs, William: Vital signs nominal. Patel, Alyssa: vital signs nominal. Benjamin, Elizabeth: vital signs nominal.*

"*McGuire, Derrick: reported deceased.*

"*Currently unable to locate Ball, Adrian; Hunt, Davis; or Shaffer, Leonard. Please approach subjects and try again.*" The computer clicked off and fell silent. Caroline looked at Liz.

"You're lucky."

Adrian slowly crawled out of the log and looked around; he was alone. He didn't know how long he'd been asleep but he felt horrible. He didn't want to be on Jurassic Earth anymore; he just wanted to go home and get killed by another human in a war-zone.

He mentally questioned the number of so many predators, wondering why they were all in the area, but his head hurt too much to think about anything other than survival. He pulled himself out of the log and tried to stand.

He felt the pain and fell back to the dirt ground.

His leg was broken!

Adrian managed to crawl further, dragging his leg behind him, until he reached a descending hill. He knew that the hill would be bad; it was worse than the one that he'd climbed up before encountering the dinosaur; but he was determined to return to the colony.

He pulled himself over the edge of the hill and began to roll down. The hill was steep and nearly vertical. Adrian wondered if it was a bad idea when he saw the cliff edge of the hill and nothingness beyond. He grabbed onto a root sticking out of the ground and stopped himself, lurching a little as his heavy body stopped.

"Please, little branch," Adrian prayed to anyone or anything that would listen, "just hold-" The branch gave away with a *snap* and Adrian rolled to the cliff. He screamed in silence as he fell. It wasn't far but it hurt nonetheless. Adrian heard something snap and wondered if his spine was alright. But that didn't matter; doctors on Earth could repair a broken spine and even get him to walk again.

All he had to do was survive. That was the task before him as he pulled himself off a pile of stones and dragged his body through the jungle. He was aware of the blood trail and knew of the dinosaurs circling him. One approached cautiously but didn't interfere with Adrian: it allowed the computer to analyze the dinosaur.

"Computer," Adrian was aware that he was coughing blood, "tell me what it is." He was panting.

"*Ornitholestes is a small carnivore with light bones. Highly intelligent; scientists suspect that it is adapted to running and hunting in packs. It can easily be identified by its stature, color, and sexual display. Ornitholestes is roughly six feet long with long, muscular legs and a thick tail tipped with rudimentary feathers. It is mainly blue but thought to change color depending on surroundings. Ornitholestes has a bony crest on the front of its skull used for purposes of identification and mating: females have crests that match their body color while males have white and red crests.*

"*Because of there size, Ornitholestes is thought to have hunted small and injured animals in packs.*" The computer clicked off.

"Injured animals." Adrian muttered. The Ornitholestes were getting closer and more brazen; it became clear that Adrian was in no position to defend against the hunting dinosaurs. The one obstacle was the armor that Adrian wore. The Ornitholestes, which were highly intelligent, knew that they'd be able to kill Adrian quickly if they could pierce his armor.

One of the predators ducked its head in toward Adrian's broken spine and bit down on a clamp. The clamp disengaged and the helm was partially released. When his breathing mask didn't activate, Adrian was forced to breathe the Jurassic air.

He coughed, once, and his lungs burned.

Ornitholestes were hunters, but they weren't above scavenging Adrian's corpse.

15

"Have they checked in yet?" Colony president, Governor Vance Tolburn, asked as he looked around the command station. Crew members sat at various consoles, looking at digital screens, silent. Tolburn walked in circles around the crew while his advisors watched. Tolburn was a toad of a man with equally short hair, but his demeanor was strong and he had a big personality. That was why the council had chosen to send him to Jurassic Earth.

"No," McNeil shook his head, "nothing."

"Be patient." Holderson said with his arms crossing his chest. His tattoos were clearly visible as he took deep breaths.

"You told me that I shouldn't worry," Tolburn turned and stormed at Holderson, "you told me that they were ready."

"They were all experienced-"

"Experience on Earth is not the same as experience on this world." Tolburn punched Holderson in the chest with his finger. It looked like an inflated sausage pressing against metal.

"They picked up my teachings fast," McNeil said, "I doubt that they've had any problems."

"Your teachings," Tolburn barked a laugh as he turned away from Holderson, "there are three species of reptiles here. Three! How many are outside the perimeter?"

"They're not reptiles," McNeil whispered as he looked away, "dinosaurs are warm-blooded."

"I don't care if they can crochet me a blanket," Tolburn shook his head angrily; "answer my question!"

"About thirty species," McNeil spoke softly, "not including aerial and nautical reptiles."

"Thirty-fucking-species," Tolburn turned away and looked around the command station, "we should've sent an experienced team out." Tolburn was shaking his head. "But I trusted your opinions."

"Governor," Holderson said, "I never promise anyone that they'll survive this place. Anything could happen; their air-supply was compromised, they ran out of fuel, they were attacked by Githraki..."

"I don't need that headache," Tolburn wagged his finger, "*that* report will not be made."

"The Githraki *are* a threat; they may be responsible. It'll be better when you recognize that."

"The council doesn't want to know that the Githraki are impeding our progress," Toburn frowned, "we needed to find a way to convince them..."

"You already know my position on the matter."

"If this is going to work, the Githraki need to relocate their fucking settlement," Tolburn tried to quiet his voice, "so that we can construct HELIOS." HELIOS was a gate like ICARUS, though much smaller, that was designed to use the pre-existing wormhole near the Githraki settlement to connect to Earth. The problem happened to be that the nearest Githraki settlement was where the colony would have to expand if HELIOS could ever be built. "The only reason I sent that squad was so that the Githraki would encounter fresh, new faces that they don't have prior history with. Maybe some Amazonas slaves will agree to work for us and not against us."

"We can get them out." Holderson said in reference to the missing squad.

"Them?" Tolburn shook his head, "I know, but the cost might not be worth it. ICARUS works for now," Tolburn's voice dropped, "but we need HELIOS to work if we hope to begin mining." He fell silent for a few second. "The council insists."

"Then we should do what we must." Holderson stood straight.

"Killing the natives is bad press," Tolburn shook his head, "the council doesn't want bad press."

"Sir?" One of the command crew turned in their swivel seat; her eyes focused on Tolburn. "You should look at this." The woman turned away and pointed at the screen. Tolburn, Holderson, and McNeil walked over.

**DETECTION: CPU DINOSAUR-IDENTIFY ACTIVATED
BEYOND RANGE
IP IDENTIFY (Y/N)?
DETECTION: CPU DINOSAUR-IDENTIFY ACTIVATED
BEYOND RANGE
IP IDENTIFY (Y/N)?**

"What is it?" Tolburn asked.

"The long-range scanner detected the use of two mini-computers," the woman said, "we can't know what information the computer accessed; but we can identify the users by their IP code."

"Who was it?" McNeil asked as he leaned forward. The woman tapped a few keys on her digital keyboard.

"Ball, Adrian and West, Caroline."

"They are co-squad leaders in the missing squad," McNeil said to Tolburn before turning back to the woman, "can you tell us anything more?"

"No," she admitted, "Ball was at the edge of our range and West was further away. Only the communicators could work any better."

"Is the squad communication device still active?" Tolburn asked.

"Yes, and within a short distance of West's computer," the woman said as she tapped a few keys, "but the comm. is not responding."

"Why not?"

Rosanna turned the communicator off as she helped Natalia. The woman had started to fall as her balance left her and the added weight of the operational communication computer hindered her movements.

Tolburn walked into his small office, with windows looking out at command central, McNeil and Holderson in tow.

"They're alive." McNeil said.

"We can't know for sure." Tolburn waved his hand dismissively.

"Adrian's computer was active," McNeil stepped beside Tolburn's desk, "and the squad's communication device is operational though not responding."

"That doesn't mean that they're alive; or that they'll remain that way." Tolburn dropped into his seat and put his head in his hands.

"Is anything heading in that area right now?"

"There's an iguana-tron moving in that direction," Holderson shrugged, "but it's a few months away."

"Can we send another Raptor?" McNeil asked.

"No," Holderson shook his head, "the council has strict orders regarding rescue. Besides, their location is not far from a known Amazonas camp." Tolburn sighed.

"Then God go with them."

16

"Let's move." Caroline said. The squad ran forward, out from the cover of the few trees at the edge of the jungle, into the open valley. John and Caroline ran together, guns on a swivel, as they moved from the trees to the cover of a small stand of broken rocks and trees. John reached the spot first and slid forward, his lower legs flat against the ground, so that he could quickly look under the hanging branches that served as a small shelter. Caroline jogged in next with Candy and Rosanna helping Natalia. Willy had the idea to make a circle with explosives near the edge of the valley to alert anyone in the area; Liz and Alyssa covered him.

"Where do we go?" Natalia asked.

"I don't even know where we are." Caroline admitted. She had been watching her computer but there was interference that kept her from mapping the area.

"We have to do something." John said softly as he looked around. An alarm went off in his head and he swung his rifle in large arcs. The other members of the squad didn't detect anything amiss but John felt the warning. Willy and Liz were still outside of the shelter, in clear view of the valley, when Alyssa screamed.

Two carnivores, eyes focused on the Diplodocus and Camptosaurs, rushed out of the jungle as a swift hunter moved through African grass. The large animals, which Caroline recognized, ignored the humans as they went after their preferred target.

"Those are the ones that tried to kill us." Caroline said, though John took it as a question.

"Yeah," John nodded and took a knee to steady his aim, "and they'll try again if they spot us."

"Everyone in the shelter," Caroline ordered as she looked at Willy and Liz. The two moved into the shelter as Alyssa took point at the shelter's edge. She dropped to her stomach and aimed the rifle at the carnivores.

"Computer," Caroline spoke softly, "can you identify?"

"*Negative; beyond communication range with the colony.*" She was even too far for the colony to detect her attempted use of the CPU.

"Rosanna," Liz whispered, "can you call the colony and tell them where we are?" Liz turned to Rosanna who was crouched in the back of the shelter with Natalia. Rosanna had forgotten about the radio and nodded. As she slung the radio off her back, she flipped the switch on the side and the radio hummed to life.

"Colony HQ, this is S.West," Rosanna spoke softly so that the carnivores wouldn't hear, "come in; Colony HQ, this is S.West..." The carnivores lunged at an elderly Camptosaurus but were immediately beaten back by the whip-like tails of several Diplodocus. The tails swung over the heads of the predators but didn't strike unless the herds were threatened.

The carnivores took a few steps back and bellowed in rage; they were determined to kill. The one that hadn't been hit with the Diplodocus tail, the younger of the two carnivores, began sniffing the air and turning its head.

"Uh-oh." John whispered.

"*This is Colony HQ, we hear you.*" The radio speaker was loud and both carnivores easily heard it. Rosanna turned the volume down as the predators stalked toward the shelter.

"Colony; S.West has been severely weakened. Dinosaurs have interfered with progress. Fatalities have occurred." Rosanna spoke fast and quiet; the carnivores were approaching.

"*Please repeat.*"

"I don't have any fucking time to repeat myself," Rosanna cursed under her helmet, "we're going to die; do you understand that?"

"*Please hold.*"

"Great," Rosanna shook her head and looked at Caroline, "they put me on hold."

"Typical bureaucratic bullshit." Caroline shook her head before turning her attention to the field. The carnivores were only a hundred yards away; they moved slowly and carefully, but there was no denying their direction.

"*This is Governor Tolburn at Colony HQ,*" the radio voice changed from a computerized female to the stern voice of the colony governor, "*what's your status?*"

"Our status is: we're fucked!"

"*How many casualties?*"

"Four," Rosanna replied quickly, "get us out of here!"

"*Is your pilot alive?*"

"Yeah," Rosanna nodded, "so?"

"*Can you fly back to the colony?*"

"Our Raptor went down," Rosanna wanted to use some 'choice' words but she restrained herself, "we had to abandon the craft."

"*Are you in any danger at this moment?*"

"That's a stupid question," Rosanna snapped as the carnivores began charging, "We're all going to die!" The carnivores roared.

John and Alyssa fired their rifles simultaneously. John's bullet struck the lead carnivore in the thigh to stop its forward momentum while Alyssa went for the head. However, John's powerful shot tripped the carnivore forward so that Alyssa's bullet ricocheted off the bone skull.

The bullet round fired back into the shelter and destroyed the radio with a bloody sizzle. There was a *crack* of electricity and a *hum* as the electronics turned off.

It left a whole in Rosanna's chest the size of a grapefruit.

"Shit." Rosanna muttered as she fell over, dead. Her blood seeped out of her where the wound wasn't cauterized. The radio sparked a few more times before it also went dead.

"FUCK, FUCK, FUCK!" Tolburn slammed the radio receiver down on the desk repeatedly. The crew officer was so frightened that she nearly fell off of her chair in fear. Tolburn eventually took a few deep breaths and gently put the receiver down. The computer had a report: no signal.

"Calm down." Holderson said, staying safely a few yards away.

"Calm down?" Tolburn turned to look at Holderson. "Are you out of your mind? There were four dead, not including the pilot. That was before the radio went dead. How many do you suppose are still alive?"

"You're going to have another hernia." Holderson kept his voice flat. Tolburn should've been sent back to Earth because of his medical condition but his influence had kept him in the Jurasssic.

"We lost a Raptor," Tolburn took several deep breaths until his heartbeat slowed, "and a high-capacity rifle. The council will understand." Tolburn knew that his own words were worthless. "HELIOS will just have to wait."

"If you'd have let me handle this in the first place," Holderson said as he changed his stance, "HELIOS would already be set." He crossed his arms behind his back and stood with his feet spread as far apart as his shoulders. He held his head high and his neck muscles were flexed.

"Is that your suggestion?"

"It is."

"The iguana-tron will get there eventually," Tolburn sighed, "send them new orders."

"What shall I say?" Holderson resisted smiling; he'd hoped for this.

"Burn the Githraki settlement, scatter them to the wind." Holderson finally smiled at Tolburn's words.

17

"The radio is shot to shit..." Willy inspected what remained of Rosanna while the other squad members watched. The carnivores were gone; the injured one had limped away while the healthy one walked behind. "Rosanna is dead." Nobody questioned that statement; it was clear that Rosanna hadn't survived the accidental gunshot.

Accident.

John wondered about his own 'accident' again. He often thought about the soldiers that he'd been responsible for. Caroline would've been there if she hadn't transferred to the Navy.

The street was quiet, only the sound of licking flames indicated that humans had ever been there. John led his team from ruined vehicle to broken wall as they maneuvered through the desolate urban zone. Intelligence had scanned the area and determined that there were no humans; but command always wanted to check. That's the reason John and his team were there.

They came to a building with a partially caved-in roof; it'd been hit by a remote drone. The building appeared deserted and was going to be bypassed when one of the soldiers heard the unmistakable sound of a child crying. Since they couldn't risk leaving a single human child behind, the team had entered the building.

That was the accident: thinking that there was a human child and not something else pretending to be human.

John shook his head to try forgetting the memory; but the injury to his face was a constant reminder that he couldn't drink away. He partly wished that his coffin had been sent adrift in deep space: he'd been entirely unaware while he was in cryo-stasis and wanted to experience that again.

Maybe they'd honor that request if the squad survived.

If they survived... that was the challenge.

"Can anything be salvaged?" Caroline asked.

"Some of her supplies," Willy said as he inspected Rosanna's belt, "but her armor and primary weapon were destroyed by the bullet."

"What about her sidearm or knife?"

"Both are intact but we're all pretty loaded up," Willy turned to Candy, "unless you want to lug more around. I noticed that you only gave Davis half of the medical supplies."

"No, thanks." Candy stuck her tongue out of her mouth but nobody could see her do it.

"I'll take the knife." John whispered. When nobody appeared to have heard him, John repeated himself.

"What about the sidearm?" Liz asked.

"You can have that," John said, "I think that the knife will be more useful."

"What do you mean?"

"Give me the knife," John's voice suddenly rose, "now!" Willy shrugged and tossed John the knife. John's own movements were fast, like a cat on steroids. He twisted the blade to the top of the shelter and sliced a metal arrow in half. The tip continued to the back of the shelter while the rest of the shaft fell at Natalia's feet.

"Damn." Natalia said.

"What the hell?" Alyssa asked.

"We're not alone out here." John lowered his arms. Everyone noticed that John's focus was on the exterior of the shelter. As one, they turned and looked. Standing over seven feet tall each, wearing clothes made from animal hide and carrying weapons of Githraki design were three Amazonas warriors.

18

Agricultural fields surrounded the Amazonas village. Females, dressed in light clothes covering their upper bodies, looked up from their work as the hovercrafts skirted above the dirt roads. Nobody was interested in the vehicles; the passengers drew stares. Only humans were visibly around though John felt the presence of Githraki.

"What're they looking at?" Alyssa asked.

"They think about a person that wears shiny skin," Jürgen, the Amazonas leader, said, "and has no face." He had to shout to be heard over the noise of the hovercrafts but the speakers in the squad helmets amplified Jürgen's words.

"Where did you learn to speak like us?" Willy asked.

"It speaks!" Jürgen laughed. "I no sure."

"He asked you a question." Liz snapped.

"The Masters are good to us." Jürgen smiled.

The hovercrafts went up a slight rise and approached the village gate. John was surprised by what he saw: massive guns on rotating axis allowed a defense of the entire area. The gate itself was made of iron bars that were currently raised; but could be dropped at a moment's notice.

A lightning bolt design on the gate signified that it could be electrified.

Amazonas warriors armed with bows and arrows patrolled the parapet while robotic arms were perched menacingly around. They watched the hovercrafts pass under the iron gate with straight faces but always kept their focus on the horizon; wary of dinosaurs.

"Where're you taking us?" John asked.

"Priest wants to see you," Jürgen said calmly, "he wants to know what your people are doing."

"Priest?" John asked.

"The one the Masters sent." Jürgen explained. John hissed.

"Githraki scum."

The Amazonas village was a patchwork of primitive buildings mixed with plate-steel provided by the Githraki. The central building, house of Priest, was conical and made of various metals. Windows provided natural light. The hovercrafts stopped in front of the conical house and Jürgen leapt from his seat. He bade the squad members to follow as he led the way inside. An arch engraved with Githraki letters 'welcomed' everyone though John didn't feel very welcomed.

A Githraki, old in their way, stood with its back facing the squad and its four arms moving wildly. It held up a hand to silence the arrivals while its other hands continued to maneuver the book that it read. Its skin was molted green and it lacked the hair-like antenna common to the Githraki. It wore little more than a light robe and a feathered headdress, something that was ceremonial in nature.

"I do not like your people," it said as it turned, "however; I *am* curious." Priest had bones that were visible under skin that was nearly translucent and its insect eyes were sunken in its narrow head. The headdress fell to the tops of the mandibles that clicked when it spoke. "What do your people plan?"

"How can you speak like us?" Caroline asked.

"I presented the first question," Priest clicked without stepping forward, "etiquette dictates that you must present the first answer."

"Our people want nothing."

"Humans always want something," Priest shook its head in a fairly comical manner, "it was the Githraki that refused to allow the human disease to spread!" It clicked rapidly and Jürgen laughed.

"We answered your question; now answer ours." Candy said.

"I wanted a direct answer, you gave me garbage. I refuse your answer."

"We gave you an answer" Caroline spoke evenly, "it's not our problem if you liked it or not."

"Very well," Priest sighed, "humans have reached for the stars for a long time. Before humans and Githraki ever met, humans were transmitting their language to the stars. When human ships tried to find new stars and new worlds to destroy... the Githraki armada waited and already knew how to speak like you. We came to this world to stop the spread of the human disease."

"There has been talk about opening another gateway back to our homeworld; but the nearby Githraki settlement prevents it."

"And they will not move; there is no need for more humans," Priest clicked as he approached, "the spread of the human disease stops here." Priest looked at John. "Githraki have seen what humans do to each other; and we intervene when necessary."

"What did your kind do to me?" John asked.

"In an attempt to kill you," Priest shook its head, "we improved upon your design." It looked at John for another moment before looking at Caroline. "Take off your helmets."

"What?!" Caroline took a step away from Priest; if Jürgen hadn't taken their weapons away, Caroline would've defended herself.

"That'll kill us." Natalia mumbled.

"I think that's the idea." Caroline said through her radio to Natalia. When the squad didn't move, Priest waved his free hands at a pair of Amazonas soldiers nearby. One of the men nodded and both ran around the corner. A silver object in the ceiling began to glow an instant before a burst of blue electricity was fired.

The computers in the squad armor were deactivated; that included the breathing devices. The servos whirred in rapid fury. There was no choice; they'd suffocate without the breathing devices.

The soldiers quickly removed their helms and were immediately assaulted by the Jurassic air. Their lungs burned and, one by one, they dropped to their knees. They were going to die after a few moments of suffering.

John coughed. He found that he was able to handle the Jurassic air better than his companions but was still suffering; he held his body up with strong arms but the crushing weight of the suit was trying to drag him down.

"The women will be slaves," Jürgen said as he approached John, "while the men are killed for fun." He kicked John's arm so that the soldier fell to the ground. John fell unconscious when his head slammed into the stone floor.

19

John woke in a circular room with barred windows. He lifted his head to see Willy lying nearby. He slowly climbed to his feet to find that most of his armor was gone, replaced with clothing similar to that worn by the Amazonas warriors. His skin was partially painted though he didn't have the elaborate decorations common to the warriors.

If he had to guess, John suspected that he was in a ritualized execution.

He was aware that his head pounded and carefully rubbed his right temple as Willy stirred. The demolition soldier rolled onto his side and vomited before he looked around. The circular room had a shallow pool in one corner with several artificial islands circling the water. A gate was drawn down on the far side of the room while the only light was provided by the overhead windows.

John's vision changed and he was able to see the blood splatter everywhere and the scattering of human bones; nobody ever seemed to survive the room. He wished he knew what was waiting for the two men.

"My head is killing me." John muttered.

"The air we're used to breathing is filled with so many chemicals that our bodies are accustomed to them," Willy explained with eyes closed, "the Jurassic air is free of those chemicals and has a greater oxygen content. Our bodies survived though it's doubtful that we can ever return to a colony building without medical intervention." His eyes eventually opened.

"We have to survive this chamber," John whispered, "before we even consider that."

"It'd be possible," Willy shook his head, "if they hadn't taken my explosives."

"All my weapons are gone, too." John frowned.

"They gave me a small knife and spear."

"Same here." John inspected the weapons. The dagger's edge was smooth and appeared ineffective while the spear handle was crooked so that it wouldn't fly straight.

"I don't think that we're meant to survive this." Willy said as the gate slowly rose. A menacing roar filled the room as a dinosaur entered with a chain around its neck. It was almost thirty-feet long and about six feet tall at the hips. It shook the ground as it walked, slowly entering the water that barely covered its three toes. It had a series of spines raising from its back and connecting a small sail to its neck, though the sail only made it appear a foot taller. Thick veins crossed the sail, making it an ineffective weapon that was more likely used for sexual display or defense. It had three, sickle shaped, claws on each hand that flexed as though it was able to easily grab it.

"What is that thing?" John asked. The dinosaur had a long snout that gave it a crocodilian appearance.

"I don't know," Willy admitted, "we've never seen it before."

"This is a gift from our Masters," Jürgen's voice came from no visible source but filled the room, "the spine lizard will kill you."

"Not if we kill it first." John said. He watched the dinosaur walk forward on powerful legs and turn to Willy. John could actually see the dinosaur's vision focus on Willy. Though it meant Willy's death, John decided to change position. When Willy screamed, unable to defend himself against the dinosaur, John rushed into the water. He ran at the dinosaur.

The carnivore lifted half of Willy's body into the sky and swallowed him whole as John approached. The water slowed him down, but it was shallow enough that John was able to move without too many problems.

The dinosaur turned its large head and roared, but John was already beneath it. He had to duck under the dinosaur's belly as he drove the dagger above his head. He ripped open the dinosaur's belly as he ran.

The dinosaur howled and tried to turn but John remained out of its reach. Blood sprayed on John and he spit to keep his mouth clear.

When the dagger was useless, John took the spear and stabbed the dinosaur in the throat. It roared just before it collapsed. It fell to the side and John avoided it, careful to stay away from the deadly feet. The last thing he wanted was to die because of another accident.

Accident.

John remembered the feeling of a green talon tearing out his right eye before he was limply thrown across the room. He was barely able to watch as the soldiers under his command were systematically disemboweled by the single greenish creature. It went to look for John after the other soldiers were dead, but John had crawled for cover and was able to hide until the alien left and help arrived.

The gate opened and a dozen Amazonas warriors rushed in; but they were hindered by the water. John didn't know why, but he felt compelled to attack the Amazonas warriors. He jumped at the nearest warrior with his limbs spread wide and landed on the warrior. He lifted the Amazonas' head and snapped his neck in a single swift move. The other Amazonas saw what happened and turned at John but the soldier was faster. He moved so fast that he was able to move without sinking below the water at all. His bare feet pivoted and he dove at another Amazonas warrior. He crushed the warrior's organs and pushed off his limp body. He landed on the last Amazonas warrior's shoulders and ripped the warrior's head off with his bare hands.

The gate started to drop but John ran from the chamber before the third Amazonas warrior was dead.

John took the stairs two at a time as he raced out of the death pit. Amazonas warriors tried to stop him but he pushed them all aside, he killed any brazen enough to get in his way by throwing them down the stone steps. He broke some necks, snapped bones, but never slowed. He reached the top floor, which was level with the ground, and ran out into the village.

Amazonas moved around, indifferent to what was happening; children played while women carried about their chores. John looked around until he saw the conical structure in the center of the camp.

He ran for it.

When he pushed open the doors, he was greeted by a dozen heavily armed Amazonas warriors while Jürgen and Priest watched from a second floor balcony.

"Tell them to leave," John said, "unless they're ready to die."

"You might kill a few," Jürgen said with a smug smile, "but you won't kill them all."

"You'll be surprised by what I can do." John laughed as the first of the warriors approached. Time seemed to slow as John dropped to one knee to intercept the warrior's lunge. He elbowed the warrior in the crotch and rose to his feet, lifting the confused warrior off the floor. When the warrior landed, John slammed his foot down and crushed the warrior's skull.

The second and third warriors flanked John, spears pointed at him, and rushed forward. Again, time slowed as the warriors moved. John looked at both and then jumped straight up in the air. He grabbed hold of a low-hanging chandelier and remained in the air while the two warriors ran into each other, impaled on the spears they carried. John dropped back to the ground, landing in a pool of blood.

The fourth warrior threw an axe, unwilling to rush John. The soldier watched the axe fly through slow time and easily grabbed the handle as it passed. John turned in a circle and threw the axe back; decapitating the warrior.

John walked forward and grabbed the fifth warrior by the neck to rip out his throat while he kicked the sixth warrior in the chest to knock him unconscious. John dropped the dead fifth warrior and looked up at the balcony.

"You did not learn." Priest said. John heard a scream as a scantily clad Liz was dragged to the balcony. Priest tied a rope around her throat and pushed the defenseless woman over the edge. John watched, unable to help, as the rope snapped taught around Liz's throat and strangled her. She was dead before the Amazonas men started laughing.

John growled when he heard the laughing.

There were six more Amazonas warriors, all partially distracted by Liz's death, near John. Their distraction was their mistake and John meticulously killed each of them. Priest growled. Natalia was dragged to the balcony, dressed like Liz, and a rope was tied around her neck. Priest pushed her off the balcony without a word.

John grabbed a sharp dagger from the nearest Amazonas warrior and threw it at Natalia. The blade skimmed her head, taking a few gold strands, and sliced through the rope. Natalia fell a dozen feet to the stone floor but she was alive.

She coughed and rubbed her throat as John stalked toward the nearest stairs. Priest watched with a depressed face.

20

When John reached the second floor the Amazonas had already fled behind Priest. He found Caroline and Alyssa, bound with gags in their mouths, but otherwise unharmed. John quickly looked around but it was clear that they were alone.

"Where're Liz and Natalia?" Alyssa asked. John looked at her and shook his head.

"Liz is dead," John said softly, "Natalia survived and is downstairs." The women looked at each other and started to stand, though they were unsteady on their feet. Caroline stumbled into John and let him hold her as she focused on his face.

"Jesus..." She whispered, forgetting that there was one woman missing.

"What is it?" John asked.

"Your eyes," Caroline backed away, "what did they do to you?" His right eye glowed soft red like that of a machine while his left eye was green with a black slit like that of a reptile. She didn't mention it, but John's entire face was twisted and alien.

"The Amazonas tried to kill me," John frowned and looked toward the empty balcony, "like they killed Willy. I hope that they enjoyed the show; I killed their dinosaur."

"They had a dinosaur?" Alyssa asked.

"Yeah," John looked at Alyssa and nodded, "it was chained up but the intent was to kill both of us."

"Could the Githraki be using the dinosaurs to attack the colony?" Alyssa asked.

"That would require them to control the dinosaurs," Caroline shrugged, "I don't know if they have that technology."

"There's no point in speculating on their technology," John thought about the rotating guns and hovercrafts, "we don't know what the Githraki are capable of." He could see the insect-faced monsters with six limbs and numerous small mouths, exoskeletons and horns. He remembered his parents talking about 'evil' when he was a child; those aliens were definitely 'evil.'

"We should go," Caroline said, purposely looking away from John, "before they come back."

"Yeah." John started to turn away when he noticed a small door in the back of the room. The writing on it was a jumbled mess; still John found that he could understand what it meant. Just inside, barely visible, was his rifle. The weapons that had been taken away were stored just a few yards from him. As the women moved to the stairs, John ran to the storage room to retrieve the weapons and bags of their supplies. When his arms were full, he turned and ran for the stairs.

He stopped at the bottom and nearly ran into Caroline. Priest had a figure-8 shaped rifle pointed at Natalia.

"I will stop the spread of the human disease before you infect another world. No more will your kind be allowed to destroy the life of the universe; you're fools if you think otherwise. You will die." Priest said.

"You won't stop us." Caroline growled. Priest smiled and turned the rifle so that it was pointed at Caroline. He noticed the bags in John's hands and turned the weapon his way.

"You were given a remarkable gift that doesn't require sacks. Drop the bags." Priest commanded.

"No." John hissed.

"Drop the bags." Caroline commanded John. John nodded slowly and carefully lowered the bags to the floor. Natalia watched and noticed a pack of cigarettes; she leaned and reached for the pack. Priest saw and instantly spun on Natalia.

"What are you doing?" Priest asked.

"I just want a smoke." Natalia said, ignoring the rifle, as she pulled the pack of cigarettes free. As she was bent over the open sacks, Natalia noticed a grenade and slid it out of the bag, careful to hide it from Priest.

"We're getting out of here." John said.

"You will try." Priest smiled and cocked the rifle with a flick of his thumb. There was a soft *hum* as the weapon's power-cells charged.

"Do me a favor," Natalia pulled a single match from her boot as she coughed blood, "get out of this place before I destroy it." She struck the match and a small flame appeared. She lit a cigarette and put it to her lips. She inhaled deeply and smiled. In her hand was the explosive.

"Run." Caroline said. John grabbed the bags as Alyssa took a step away. Priest's reptilian eyes grew wide as he pulled the trigger. It shot Natalia in the shoulder but the pilot didn't seem concerned. She inhaled again as she pulled the grenade's safety clip. She exhaled and lifted the grenade to her mouth.

The soldiers turned and ran as a spark from Natalia's cigarette ignited the grenade's trigger. Priest was unable to run as a massive explosion consumed everything. Natalia was dead before she could feel pain but Priest suffered.

The soldiers ran to the nearby hovercrafts and jumped in. John threw the bags in as he pulled his rifle free. Amazonas warriors ran at them but John shot them, disintegrating their vital organs. The Amazonas may have been taller and faster, but John wasn't human anymore.

"John!" Caroline cried as Alyssa activated the hovercraft's engine. John jumped into the silver vehicle and, after stowing his rifle, casually drew a sonic explosive out of a bag. He grinned, baring razor-sharp teeth, as he flicked the explosive into the other hovercraft. The impact of the explosive hitting the hovercraft was enough to activate it.

The second hovercraft was destroyed as a pair of Amazonas warriors attempted to climb into it. They were killed as shrapnel tore their flesh.

Alyssa pushed the throttle down and the hovercraft darted forward. Metal arrows flew at the fleeing vehicle but John, with only a dagger in his hand, moved at blinding speed to deflect the poisonous shafts. In mere seconds, Alyssa forced the hovercraft out of the village and into the farm fields. A laser bolt, fired from one of the rotating guns, struck the back of the hovercraft and ignited one of the engines.

The hovercraft continued away from the village's borders with smoke trailing behind it. Alyssa pushed the alien craft as far as it would go until the engines quit and the surviving soldiers were required to walk.

21

The bellowing of various dinosaurs filled the sky as the sun set. Caroline led the way as John and Alyssa followed with their weapons at the ready. They had put on a lot of their armor but kept their helmets off; they'd suffocate without working computers. John knew that humans were capable of many atrocities but he didn't believe that the Githraki were benevolent supporters of the universe; in John's opinion, the Githraki were entirely evil.

A single dinosaur with a shell-like back and spikes between its back and soft underbelly lumbered nearby as it foraged on the low bushes. A rumble on the horizon announced an approaching storm. Brief flashes of lightning highlighted the graceful necks of large sauropods.

"Do you think it's possible," Alyssa asked, "that the Githraki could use dinosaurs against our colony?"

"I think that the Githraki hate us enough to try." Caroline replied in a hushed voice. The armored dinosaur looked at them and swung its flat tail, though it was hardly disturbed by the presence of humans.

"We should find some shelter before the rain starts." John said as he looked at the sky. He was aware that acid wouldn't be falling, a stark reminder that he wouldn't be home, but he was in no mood to get wet.

"I agree," Caroline said, "let's head for those trees." She turned and the trio headed for the cover of the canopy. Once under the trees it wasn't hard to find a fallen log and arrange various branches and ferns for added protection. It wouldn't stop a hungry carnivore, but it would keep the rain away.

"What next?" Alyssa asked after the shelter was built. They had worked in silence though John's movements were noticeably different than normal.

"We each take a shift guarding the shelter," Caroline said, "while the others rest. I'll take first shift, then John, then you." She looked at Alyssa. "Do you have a problem with that?"

"No, ma'am." Alyssa replied instantly. John said nothing.

"Good," Caroline nodded, "let's do it."

Night fell quietly but insistently; the darkness was absolute. When Caroline disappeared behind a large tree, John sat and looked at the stars. He imagined that he could see ICARUS but that was impossible. He could foresee ICARUS drifting into space, unused, as the Githraki settlement became the primary method of transportation between Earth and Jurassic Earth.

John slowly climbed to his feet and stepped away from the camp, his motions casting strange shadows in the flickering firelight. Fire kept predators away; survival training taught them all that much.

Caroline had posted herself outside of the firelight, a short distance away from the camp, on a small hill so that she could watch the entire area. John approached quietly; Caroline didn't notice him until he was a few steps away.

"Christ," Caroline took a few deep breaths, "you nearly scared the shit out of me!" She stammered.

"I made it close," John spoke softly; "it's a good thing that I wasn't coming to kill you." He was smiling but it was hard to see in the darkness. His right eye was visible; his red eye.

"Is it time for me to go to sleep?" Caroline asked. John didn't move. Caroline stood but didn't walk away. "What happened?" She asked.

"What do you mean?" John looked at her.

"I know that war is Hell; but it wasn't Hell that changed you."

"I never told you what happened in Afghanistan," he shook his head; it was still a few hours before it was his turn to watch the perimeter, "when we were attacked by a Githraki ambusher." The military had designated various Githraki warriors: Githraki marines were typical Githraki with weaponry attached to their bodies and only two arms; Githraki scouts were thin Githraki that were very agile and able to use any weapons that they encountered; Githraki mercenaries, like Priest, were solo-warriors trained in hand-to-hand combat; and then there were the Githraki ambushers that worked alone and set traps against their enemies.

"Is that what happened to your face?" Caroline asked as she turned her body to face John.

"My DNA was changed," John explained, "and I don't know what I'm capable of anymore." He was whispering, forcing Caroline to remain close.

"What're you talking about?" Caroline flicked the safety to the 'off' position and carefully moved the rifle in John's direction.

"I'm not human." John whispered as he approached her.

Caroline crawled into the camp; her clothes dirty, and fell beside Alyssa. The sniper woke and looked at the squad leader with tired eyes. Alyssa noticed Caroline's condition and frowned.

"Is everything alright?" Alyssa asked.

"Yes." Caroline only managed a weak whisper.

"What happened?" Alyssa propped herself up on her elbows and looked at Caroline while the suit struggled to give Alyssa support.

"Get some sleep," Caroline muttered, "I'm fine." Alyssa shrugged and rolled over. Caroline looked away as silent tears welled in her eyes.

On the hill, John sat in the darkness. He looked at his hands, his fingernails replaced with claws, wondering.

"What's happening to me?" John asked the night. He closed his eyes and leaned back against a broken log. He was aware of the bones protruding from his back, trying to break through the armor in pain, but he didn't care; he just wanted everything to be over. He ran his fingers over his pistol and contemplated suicide again.

Four hours passed before Alyssa arrived on the hill with the broken tree. She looked around and saw John leaning against the tree, holding a pistol in one hand and an empty cartridge in the other. She opened her mouth to speak but fell silent; he'd clearly been crying and she chose not to say anything. John was sleeping and Alyssa decided to let him stay that way while she kept watch over the camp.

22

"Sir!" The early morning sun came in the windows of the colony building but the crew was busy with their work. Satellites detected a massive explosion in the nearby Amazonas village with no clear cause, now infrared had detected something unexpected. Tolburn crossed the room, carrying a cup of coffee that he occasionally drank from, and stopped next to the crew member that had called him.

"What is it?" He asked and took another swig of mud.

"Three humanoid life-forms are moving in this direction." The crew member, a nervous woman who didn't dare look at Tolburn, said in a squeaky voice.

"Amazonas?"

"I don't think so," the woman explained, "they're wearing colony armor with ID tags hidden in them."

"Who are they?" Tolburn stopped drinking. The woman tapped a few keys on the board in front of her and a second screen lit up beside the one she had been monitoring. After a few seconds, the appropriate names were listed.

"Squad Leader Caroline West; Scout John Deacon, and Sniper Alyssa Patel."

"Where are they?"

"They're nearing the moving iguana-tron." It was only because of the iguana-tron that the colony was able to detect the surviving members of the squad.

"Can we communicate with them?"

"I've tried raising them," the woman said, "but they're not responding. We'll have to wait until they meet up with the iguana-tron."

"Why aren't they communicating?"

"Their radio could be damaged or, if I were to guess, they've turned their communication system off."

"If they turned their communication system off, how can they talk to each other?"

"I don't know, sir." Tolburn was angry but glad that there were survivors; still, he was curious.

"What about the rest of the squad?"

"I don't know."

"Good work." Tolburn patted the woman on the shoulder and quickly walked back to his office. He sat down at his desk and pressed a few buttons near the chair. A com-link activated and allowed him to speak directly to the communications office.

"*Yes?*" The electronic voice asked.

"Summon McNeil and Holderson," Tolburn said, "I want them here ASAP."

"*Sir, yes sir.*" The com-link went silent as Tolburn reclined in his chair. He took a deep gulp of coffee and closed his eyes.

Holderson stalked through the station, face grim, as he secured the few straps on his MK suit. As he neared the airlock, the armor hissed as air jetted out. He signaled to the soldier that was waiting for him: he was ready.

The small shuttle disconnected from the station and dropped into the Jurassic Earth atmosphere at a speed that would kill most humans. Holderson was fully capable of surviving while wearing the protective white body suit. As clouds rippled around the drop ship, Holderson willed his eyes open so that he could see.

The drop ship flew above endless jungle as it approached the colony a few miles away. The robotic pilots monitored the drop ship's movements as the craft soared through the sky. Holderson removed his helmet and secured the facemask so that he could breathe.

The drop ship landed a few hundred yards away from the colony headquarters and Holderson was allowed to depart. Once he was on the pavement, the shuttle rose into the sky to return to the station. It would come back to the colony if Holderson called for it.

McNeil rubbed the stubble on his chin while he looked at the Camarasaurs. They were starting to get aggressive; their mating season was approaching. He glanced at the nearby Ceratosaurus and frowned; the dinosaur had a clamp around its jaws to keep it from making any sound: Ceratosaurs had been detected near the colony but none had approached.

Now that Tolburn was calling, McNeil assumed that the time had come to eliminate the Ceratosaurus. He didn't like that idea: he wanted a carnivore present to introduce to the new arrivals. The Camarasaurs and Stegosaurus were alright; but a carnivore would inspire fear.

"Sir," a soldier standing a few yards away, "did you hear me?"

"Yeah," McNeil replied in a shallow voice, "I'm going." He glanced up to see the silhouette of a shuttle passing through the sky: he wasn't expecting new soldiers so that meant Holderson had come to the colony. He wondered why as he turned away from the dinosaurs.

He waved to a soldier in black as he headed toward the nearby doors. The soldier approached quickly.

"Sir?"

"Keep an eye on the Camarasaurs," McNeil said, "have them separated if they become violent."

"As you wish, sir." The soldier saluted McNeil who departed. McNeil entered the nearest set of doors and quickly ascended the stairs in front of him. He entered the long lobby of the colony building and saw Holderson walking in the doors opposite him.

"What's going on?" McNeil asked.

"I hoped that you'd know." Holderson said as he removed his facemask.

"Did Tolburn call you?"

"No," Holderson shook his head, "communications called."

"Same here." McNeil shrugged as both men entered the colony offices. They dodged soldiers and entered the observation room where Tolburn's office was. Tolburn was in his office, slumped in his seat with an empty coffee mug standing on his big belly. Holderson knocked on the doorframe and Tolburn's eyes opened.

"What's up?" Holderson knew that he wouldn't be called away from the station unless it was absolutely necessary; there were other commanding officers to handle the colony.

"Our missing squad is returning," Tolburn said, "I want you both present when they call in."

"They haven't called yet?"

"They're not communicating and we don't know why," Tolburn sat up and sent the coffee cup crashing to the floor, "so we have to wait."

23

The iguana-tron lumbered through the dense jungle, forcibly pushing trees out of the way as the driver pushed the throttle forward. A glass panel in front of the driver protected the cautious worker from the gigantic insects of the region. He wore goggles and kept his head on a swivel, watching the trees that arced over the black mechanical monstrosity like a broken arch.

"We've got movement." A bipedal tank, twice the size of a man, walked beside the iguana-tron with an oversized rifle in its hands. The woman controlling the tank stopped and looked around but the jungle was so thick that it was impossible to pierce the greenery. The woman tried to see what was coming despite the difficulty, her radar was beeping. She took a deep breath and steadied herself, ready to kill anything that burst through the trees; her hand moved over the control for the cannon under the right arm. The soldiers in MKII suits looked around, nervous.

"What've you got?" The driver radioed the tank pilot.

"Incoming," the pilot glanced at her radar before looking back at the jungle, "fifty yards and closing."

"Dinosaurs?" The driver's voice shook in fear as he pulled the throttle back.

"Negative." She gulped and hoped that there weren't any dinosaurs. She waited as a series of branches were pushed aside by the unknown force. She froze and looked, human soldiers were quickly approaching. She lowered the rifle as a human male appeared with a black gun pointed in her direction. His rifle looked like the one carried by the tank, though smaller with strange blue patterns along the barrel. Two women slowly followed, both equipped with guns standard for colony soldiers.

"It's the iguana-tron," one of the women said to the others, "we're closer." The iguana-tron driver noticed that the humans weren't wearing face masks.

"Lower your weapons and identify yourselves." The tank pilot spoke through a PA system so that the three humans could hear her. The human male had his rifle trained on the tank but slowly lowered it as the iguana-tron's various weapons turned in his direction.

"I'm Caroline West," one of the women that ran out of the jungle said, "squad leader." She was thin, somewhat emaciated, and dirty. Caroline pointed to her female companion. "This is Alyssa Patel, our squad sniper." Alyssa was slightly shorter than Caroline with eyes that were designed to automatically focus on her targets. Like all snipers, she wore a band on her right arm that kept drugs in her blood so that her aim was never off even if her armor was compromised. "That is John Deacon." John was the male with the strange rifle. He was dressed in the grey armor like the other human soldiers, though the right half of his face was scarred and the eye was blank. He had a stern face and was cautious in his movements.

"What happened to you?" The driver asked through a similar PA system.

"It's a long story," Alyssa replied quickly but Caroline didn't appear to mind, "but we're eager to get back to the colony."

"Wait a moment," the driver spoke calmly as he pressed a few keys on his dash. He turned the PA system off before he opened a communication line with the colony.

"IT Seven-Seven-Four to Laurasia HQ." It took a few moments for the colony to answer his call.

"*Laurasia Colony,*" the robotic voice answered, "*ready for communication.*"

"This is Herbert Franklin," the driver said, "iguana-tron driver dispatched by the colony. Three human soldiers have been discovered."

"*Provide the names of the discovered.*" The robot said.

"West, Patel, and Deacon." Franklin had to think for a moment as the names came to him. The communicator was silent for a few seconds before a response was sent.

"*Please hold for Governor Tolburn.*"

"Wow," he tapped another button and turned the PA system back on, "you've got the attention of the colony governor."

"We were carrying out an important mission for the colony," Caroline said though her companions were silent of the exact details, "the governor should be interested."

Tolburn jumped from his desk and dashed into the communications room as fast as his short legs could manage; McNeil and Holderson on his heels. For an apathetic man, Tolburn could move when necessary. Holderson leaned against the doorframe of the communications room while McNeil took a few steps inside. Tolburn sat at an empty desk and slid the microphone so that it was inches from his lips.

"This is Governor Tolburn," Tolburn said eagerly, "please identify yourself."

"*Franklin, Herbert. Registered iguana-tron driver and certified pilot; ID: Juno-Alpha-Nike-Echo-Typhon-Orphan-Niner. Operating IT Seven-Seven-Four.*" The response was immediate. One of the nearby secretaries nodded, confirming the contact source. Her computer screen showed Franklin's Identification File and picture.

"What's your status?"

"*We're about a half-click away from the border river; progress was made easier by thin sections of the jungle.*"

"What's your distance from the colony?"

"*Approximately seven clicks.*" It was actually 7.2 miles.

"What's your report?"

"*Three human soldiers from the colony have been identified.*"

"Who have you located?"

"*West, Caroline. Patel, Alyssa. Deacon, John.*" There was a moment of hesitation. Tolburn looked at Holderson and McNeil.

"The other members of that squad are still MIA."

"Or KIA." McNeil whispered, saying only that which the others already thought.

"What's the condition of the human soldiers?" Tolburn turned back to the microphone.

"*They're semi-emaciated, dirty, and weak. They show some signs of combat, though it's not clear if it resulted from dinosaur influence.*" It went unsaid that the Githraki were likely responsible.

"Are you carrying a medical pod?"

"*This is an iguana-tron, sir; of course.*"

"If possible, send the survivors back to the colony via the medical pod before continuing to your objective."

"*Understood.*"

"Make contact again if there's a problem," Tolburn said with a straight face, "otherwise, we'll anticipate them."

"*There is something I should mention,*" there was a pause, "*they're not wearing breathing masks.*" Tolburn's eyes went wide and he turned to Holderson while cupping the microphone.

"Can they survive without breathing masks?" Tolburn asked. Holderson though for a silent moment before meeting Tolburn's gaze.

"Yes," Holderson nodded slowly, "though it's complicated."

"How so?"

"Imagine being underwater for an extended period of time," Holderson explained, "divers have to rise slowly to reduce the amount of nitrogen in their blood. This is reverse; too little nitrogen with an abundance of oxygen. The results will be similar and equally deadly."

"Can the medical teams help them?"

"Yes," Holderson said after a short pause, "though nobody has died from the bends in over fifty years so I doubt that they have experience in the matter."

"Alright," Tolburn said solemnly before turning back to the microphone and removing his hand, "can you still hear me?"

"*Sir; yes sir.*"

"Send the survivors back to the colony," Tolburn said, "just be sure that the medical pod's air regulators are deactivated. We'll have the medical teams ready. Understood?"

"*Understood.*"

Franklin turned off his communicator and frowned; he knew that the survivors were walking corpses. It was just a matter of time before they died; it was a wonder if they even knew. Franklin sighed.

"You're going to the colony where you'll be treated for your medical... injuries," Franklin announced, "use the medical pod in the iguana-tron's tail. Do you understand me?"

"We do." Caroline replied quickly. Franklin noticed that the male soldier never looked at the iguana-tron while the woman appeared eager to leave.

"Good," Franklin tapped a few keys and the air regulators in all of the medical pods were deactivated, "you'll be expected." An alarm flashed as the iguana-tron's tail opened and the medical pod slowly slid out from the internal chamber it was stored in. The alarm continued to blare and a red light flashed but Franklin ignored it.

24

The medical pod raced along the trail made by the iguana-tron and the bipedal tank, its thin legs moving so fast that the limbs were nearly invisible. It automatically followed the straight trail created by the black tank. It was similar in design to the Amazonas hovercrafts; though the medical pod was black and was large enough to carry a bipedal tank. The three survivors had room to sit and stretch out while they returned home.

"I'll make sure that a memorial is built," Caroline whispered, "to honor our fallen comrades."

"What'll it say?" Alyssa asked.

"Adrian Ball, Davis Hunt and Leonard Shaffer; presumed dead." Nobody had said anything about Adrian's group surviving and Liz had been adamant that their survival was unlikely. "Rosanna Lewis, Derrick McGuire, Natalia Whitley, William Hobbs, and Elizabeth Benjamin; killed in the line of duty."

"What about Candy?" John never looked at his female companions. "You don't presume Candy dead; and we're not aware that she was killed."

"I hope that she's still alive," Alyssa muttered, "after what happened."

"What happened?" John looked at Alyssa.

"The Amazonas wanted to torture all of us," Caroline felt a tear roll down her cheek, "though they only took Candy away before you arrived."

"They made Candy a slave?" John's left eye went wide. "We left her?"

"We fled with our lives," Caroline corrected John, "besides; we don't know where they took Candy."

"She's alive..." John's voice faded away.

"I hope." Alyssa nodded.

"We hope." Caroline said.

"We should go back for her." John looked up.

"We'll get new supplies and bring an army with us when we return to the Amazonas village," Caroline smiled, "and we'll burn that place to the ground." It was a promise that she intended to keep.

Candy was hanging in an empty room, her hands bound together while she dangled from the ceiling. Her pink hair was ragged, fallen in front of her face, and her light skin was stained with dirt smeared by tears.

"Your allies have left you for dead, what do you think of that?" An elderly Githraki woman, her green skin wrinkled and her tendril 'hair' receding, asked with a toothless smile. She laughed while she spoke, her mandibles clicked. Candy was slightly amused.

"She asked you a question." Jürgen sat in a chair with his arms and legs crossed. He had been drinking blue syrup but his cup was empty.

"I'll never be forgotten." Candy whimpered.

"They forgot about you as they ran for their lives." Jürgen laughed. The old Githraki woman cackled and smiled; she had a single green tooth that Candy was determined to destroy.

"Laugh if you want," Candy groaned, "you'll get what's due."

"I think not," Jürgen rose to his feet and approached Candy, "your people will die soon."

"How?" Candy asked softly and spit on Jürgen.

Jürgen frowned, wiped the spittle away, and then proceeded to use Candy as a punching bag. The Githraki woman watched with a smile on her face.

"The humans will suffer like you suffer; their death has been long overdue."

The medical pod passed a tall, iron pole that marked the outer boundary of the colony. The pod automatically slowed as it reached an electrified fence a short quarter-mile later, an opening in the fence allowed the pod to proceed. The outer reaches of the colony were agricultural domes that provided food to the colonists and soldiers, while housing was closer to the center. Paved roads crossed the colony like a child's sketch.

Few people were about while machines occupied the roads; driven remotely by colonists safely confined in the utilitarian buildings. The pod was another machine, ignored even as it approached the central colony building and the landing strip.

The pod was automatically directed toward the far end of the building where the loading docks were located. The pod brought the survivors as close to the medical bays as possible without actually going through one of the walls.

"We're home." Caroline said.

"Not all of us." John muttered.

"Candy will return," Caroline whispered, "eventually." Alyssa was silent as she followed Caroline. John stopped walking and looked at the blue sky; he sighed.

"Eventually."

25

The three survivors were put in separate rooms with white walls and thick glass though the same surgery was issued to all three. They had to strip and lay on their stomachs, their bodies pressed against cold gurneys, while straps held them in place. Medical doctors moved carefully but quickly, they couldn't stay in the chambers too long. A computer guided needle was inserted in the base of the survivors' spines. While the survivors screamed in pain, a chemical to restore the health of their bodies was injected while infectious fluid was drawn out of the spine.

The medics had to be careful with Alyssa since her blood had high levels of chemicals to make her a better sniper. The medics couldn't inject the normal medicines into her since there would be dangerous side-effects.

John posed a different problem since his body didn't seem to show any sign of exposure to Jurassic Earth; he even managed to destroy three needles that were supposedly indestructible.

Caroline and Alyssa were wheeled into a metal room in the medical bay while John was moved to a different room. The women had to adjust to the oxygen levels in the colony while John was put in a holding cell; the doctors didn't know what was wrong but John was clearly different.

"What're you doing to me?" John snapped as the prison door was slammed shut. A uniformed soldier, wearing black, stood opposite John with a blank face. The guard was silent as John began to pace his cell. He punched a wall, leaving a massive dent but didn't break through, and ripped a bar out of the door though the guard didn't appear fazed.

Another door opened and the solid figure of General Holderson appeared. John stopped pacing and snapped to attention. Holderson walked up to the prison door and silently inspected the artificial hole without ever looking at John. The guard, who was also saluting, took a few steps away from the cell and relaxed his body a little as John stiffened his posture.

"I have some questions for you, soldier." Holderson said while continuing to inspect the door.

"Sir." John replied without moving his 'normal' eyes.

"At ease," Holderson said though he hardly moved, "I've seen wood more relaxed than you."

"Sir." John was formal even as his body loosened.

"Do you know where you are?"

"The Laurasia Colony."

"Do you know the date?"

"It's irrelevant," John answered, "any day is good to die." That was a standard response that all soldiers knew. Holderson smiled inwardly.

"Do you know who sits on the council?"

"Several idiots who never came to this Hell." John was unmoving while Holderson looked at John. The soldier's responses were expected though Holderson was silent for a few seconds.

"Can you tell me what happened out there?"

"We were captured by Amazonas warriors and tortured by the Githraki; only three of us escaped with our lives."

"Did the Amazonas kill everyone?"

"No," John admitted as he crossed his hands behind his back and stood with his feet shoulder-width apart, "some dinosaurs were responsible."

"How many Amazonas did you kill?"

"Several," John said without a hint of a smile, "they didn't stand a chance."

"How many Githraki died because of you?"

"We only ever saw one; it died."

"The computer in your armor recorded some of these events," Holderson turned away and walked with his head held high, "but they don't tell the whole story." He quickly turned back to face John. "What happened to your masks?"

"The Githraki demanded to see our faces," John answered, "we were forced to breathe Jurassic air. They used an electronic weapon to disable our internal computers."

"Your companions received medical treatment for the air," Holderson said, "but you did not need the aid. The air had no affect on your body." He watched John for a reaction but didn't notice one.

"I don't understand that, sir."

"Not only that," Holderson continued speaking, "but your blood tests revealed foreign DNA in your system. Can you explain that?"

"I..." John had an idea but he didn't know if he could tell Holderson the truth.

"What happened to you in Afghanistan?" Holderson asked, "What did the Githraki do to you?" John looked at Holderson but remained silent for a few seconds before answering.

"How did you know about the Githraki?"

"Your injury told me a lot," Holderson said without showing emotion, "you confirmed my suspicions."

"What do you mean?"

"Experiments were carried out at a military facility in Nevada over a century ago, prior to the forming of the White City. The Githraki that were experimented upon escaped, destroying the facility and making half of North America a dead-zone before their escape from the planet," Holderson turned away, "a lot of scientists were killed by natural alien weapons. The wounds looked like the injury on your face. The station medics informed me of the extent of your injury and what they managed to do," Holderson was pacing while avoiding John's cell, "afterwards; I monitored your progress, including your uncanny proficiency with weaponry. Now your blood tests show DNA that is known to be Githraki. Are you going to tell me what happened?"

"I led a squad of soldiers into a building that was supposed to be abandoned," John's voice dropped, "where we were all attacked by a Githraki ambusher. I was hit in the face by a hooked claw appendage and thrown aside while the rest of the squad was systematically eliminated. I crawled into hiding before the ambusher could locate me; I assume the thing wanted to kill me, but it had to escape. We were discovered by another squad; I... I couldn't attend the funerals of the dead, despite my requests, because of the extent of my injuries." John would've cried if he was able too.

"It changed you, correct?"

"The cyber-eye that the medics installed has changed the way I see the world." John nodded. Holderson noted that John didn't answer the question.

"I'm going to be petitioning your release," Holderson said after a few moments, "because I want you active if the Githraki attack." John appreciated the action though he didn't want to encounter the Githraki again. "You're a good soldier, I'd hate to lose you."

"What about Caroline and Alyssa?" John asked.

"What about them?" Holderson stopped pacing and looked at John. He avoided John's alien cut on purpose.

"Will they be released?"

"They have to finish the decompression," Holderson said, "then they'll be temporarily allowed back into service. They'll aid the colony as long as they can."

"What does that mean?"

"The doctors believe that there will be extensive mental effects that can't be predicted," Holderson said, "if the result is too bad, they'll both be removed from service."

"They won't like that."

"I don't care." Holderson's face was hard.

"I have some news," the nurse said while standing on the opposite side of a glass wall, "that your blood tests revealed." Caroline and Alyssa were sitting inside a white decompression chamber with cots and meal storage containers. The women looked at each other before looking at the nurse.

"What is it?" Caroline asked. The nurse looked momentarily uncomfortable, shifting back and forth on her feet as though she didn't want to say much. "What is it?" Caroline asked again.

"You're three weeks pregnant," the nurse finally said, looking away.

"Which one of us?" Caroline asked. The nurse looked up at Caroline and focused on the woman.

"You."

"Can you tell who the father is?" Alyssa asked as Caroline looked away.

"Since it's someone that has a medical file here in the colony; yes."

"Who?"

"John Deacon."

"Caroline West is pregnant," Holderson said as John's cell was unlocked, "that's something we're concerned about. But there's something else..."

"What?" John asked, concerned.

"According to the blood tests," Holderson hesitated, "you're the father."

26

John stood in the doorway but didn't speak. The computer screens were illuminated but the florescent lights were off. The last time he'd seen that room, the squad's meeting room, it had been filled with soldiers eager for war. Most were dead, unaware that they'd ever be missed.

"Hail to the glorious dead," John whispered a standard military memorial, "what a crock." He lifted a mug to his lips and swallowed hard liquor. John was wearing black pants, black boots with buckled straps, a black shirt, and a black jacket that drooped to his knees. He swallowed more liquor.

"How're you feeling?" Holderson walked up the hall, his boots clicking on the floor, and stopped a few steps away from John.

"I want to go home." John said without turning.

"You're already home," Holderson said, "Unless you want to go back to Earth." He paused. "I can authorize your transfer."

"I'd be out of this Hell." John nodded.

"You'd leave your child behind."

"Maybe it'd be better if they don't know me," John whispered, "I'm not much of a role model."

"You're still the father."

"I know," John sighed, "please don't remind me."

"Are you sure about this?" John turned and looked at Holderson. The day before, Governor Tolburn had announced that a new colony would be built once HELIOS was operational. Volunteers would be needed. John requested a permanent transfer. If he couldn't go home, he'd like to get away from Caroline.

"Yes." John nodded.

"West could be transferred; I hope that you know that?"

"You could also forbid their transfer," John looked away from Holderson and back into the room, "anything to keep us separate."

"I'd hate to lose you."

"You'll survive without me here."

"There is something that we have to discuss," Holderson said, "as a possibility."

"What's that?" John drank more.

"The law states that a married couple can only have two children; and a parent can only be single if their partner dies. There aren't any real exceptions."

"So?"

"If West gives birth," Holderson said, "you have to marry that woman. A child must have two parents."

"I don't have to marry her if she doesn't give birth?" It was a question though Holderson didn't hear it that way.

"That's correct." Holderson nodded.

"What am I to do then?" Typically, a single parent could 'pay' for their illegitimate child by willingly serving in the military; but since both parents were soldiers...

Holderson read John's mind, "There is another way; though it's hard to fathom."

"What's that?" John turned; he wasn't aware of another option.

"The single parent *and* child are put into cryo-stasis and sent through ICARUS. If left here, they'd be forced to enter the Gondwana swamps. But since they'd be destined for Earth, their sentence would to be exile to the America wasteland."

"That's certain death!" John turned and nearly splashed his drink on the wall.

"I told you that the option would be hard to fathom."

"That's a piss-poor option."

"Go to the colony chapel and pray," Holderson walked up to John and put a comforting hand on his shoulder, "you should do it before you drink too much to walk."

Caroline stood in the chamber's small bathroom and stared into the mirror. Alyssa was in the main room, sleeping on her cot, while Caroline pretended to shower. She ran the water to confuse the monitoring computer, but Caroline wanted to think. With a hand on her belly, Caroline weighed the options.

Abortion meant that the child wouldn't be forced to suffer and John would be able to rest easily. Caroline would suffer: she'd be stripped of her position, her weapons would be taken away, and she'd be exiled to the swamps deep in the south. She could be eaten by a dinosaur or, more likely, suffocate without a proper breathing mask.

Caroline continued to think as she looked at her face in the mirror. A monster was growing inside of her; that was the only explanation that made any sense. A monster made with John's deformed DNA. She took a deep breath and frowned; she didn't know what to do.

She turned the water off and opened the medicine cabinet above the sink. She reached for her toothbrush when she noticed a white bottle. The bottle contained the same chemicals that Alyssa had been injecting over the past several weeks to keep her sniper skills sharp. A large warning label was printed on one side; Caroline couldn't resist reading.

WARNING

EXTREME HAZARD
ONLY TAKE PRESCRIBED AMOUNT
DO NOT BREAK CAPSULE
DO NOT CHEW
DO NOT MIX CHEMICAL INGREDIENTS
USE CARE WHEN OPERATING HEAVY MACHINERY
MAY HAVE ADVERSE AFFECTS ON CHILDREN
STOP USE IF SIGNS OF EARLY PUBERTY ARE NOTICED IN
CHILDREN
IT IS VERY IMPORTANT THAT YOU TAKE OR USE THIS
EXACTLY AS DIRECTED
DO NOT SKIP A DOSE OR DISCONTINUE UNLESS
DIRECTED BY A MEDICAL PROFESSIONAL
INFORM MEDICAL IF YOU ARE PREGNANT PRIOR TO
TAKING.

Caroline bit her lower lip softly as she placed the bottle back on the shelf. She got her toothbrush and closed the cabinet door. She had to do more thinking.

27

Franklin gritted his teeth as he squeezed the trigger. The iguana-tron lurched forward as it fired a barrage of rockets across the valley. Though it wasn't likely that they'd survive; Herbert Franklin and the tank pilot Christina Hodges were going to fight until their last breath.

Christina, who'd been on point since the human survivors had been discovered, spotted the dinosaurs first and had warned Franklin of the impending doom. Allosaurs, three of them, crossed the valley with their jaws open wide and talons extended. Their roar was deafening; the ground vibrated.

"Can you raise the colony?" Christina radioed Franklin. Both were covered in sweat and beaten by exhaustion but neither was ready to quit.

"I've got to boost the signal," Franklin growled as he launched more missiles, "I need some time."

"It's asking a lot," Christina aimed her rifle at a speedy Allosaurus and fired, knocking the carnivore to the ground, "but a Raptor would be appreciated."

"Hold them off," Franklin was spitting as he spoke, "let me raise my antenna." He pushed the iguana-tron back a step and set the mechanical beast's feet in the ground. A panel in the iguana-tron's back opened and a twenty-foot tall needle rose into the sky. "Calling Laurasia Colony HQ on the Emergency Line!"

He repeated the call several times as the Allosaurs began fanning apart. The fallen dinosaur had managed to get back on its feet though it limped and blood dripped from lacerations on its legs. Franklin called again but he was starting to feel hopeless.

"*This is the colony headquarters; Emergency frequency. Identify and report.*" The response finally came. Franklin hardly heard the radio over the pounding of his own heartbeat.

"Franklin, Herbert and Hodges, Christina; we're under attack from dinosaur adversaries one click East of the nearest Amazonas settlement." Franklin spoke rapidly.

"Please repeat." The robotic voice said.

"I am Herbert Franklin, iguana-tron driver, with Christina Hodges; we're under attack from multiple dinosaur adversaries; approximately one click East of the nearest Amazonas settlement." He forced himself to swallow the curse threatening to exit his lips.

"Stay calm, Herbert Franklin; please stand-bye." Franklin shook his head when the reply came; he wasn't surprised. A similar situation had happened when he was serving in the army during the conflict against the China Republic. He'd barely survived that event.

"Great." Franklin muttered.

"What is it?" Christina radioed when she heard the concern in Franklin's voice. She paused, temporarily ceasing the raining death against the Allosaurs, and turned the tank in the direction of the iguana-tron.

"I'm on hold." He said without surprise. Christina shrugged when she was struck by a rushing Allosaurus. The tank was pushed over and the carnivore ripped the canopy away. As Christina struggled to slide her face mask on, the Allosaurus grabbed her with its powerful jaws and ripped her from the tank. It threw her to the ground and kicked the tank aside.

Christina landed in some brush and tried to crawl to safety when the three claws on the Allosaurus' hind foot crushed her and pushed her stomach into the ground. It grabbed her head in its jaws and pulled until Christina's spine broke apart.

The dinosaurs tore at her small carcass while Franklin watched in horror. He pressed a button on the dash and a targeting computer clicked on. The computer automatically locked on the nearest Allosaurus. The dinosaur turned to bloody mist when the single missile struck it in the hip. The other carnivores watched but made no move at Franklin.

"I haven't got all night!" Franklin growled.

"Be patient," a voice filled Franklin's ears though he couldn't identify the source, "unless you're eager to die."

"Who's there?" Franklin asked softly but he was confident that the question was heard.

"We are creeping chaos," the voice replied with a laugh, "and now we become your death!"

"We?"

"You'll know very soon."

"Where are you?" He was only slightly aware that the Allosaurs were again moving in his direction.

"Here." Across the valley, a metal platform hovered into view with a green man at the central controls, its four arms moving rapidly; it was a Githraki warrior. The square platform, roughly four feet wide each side with a vertical podium in the center where the Githraki warrior controlled the movements, allowed the figure to look over the trees. Tied to the platform, with a gag in her mouth, was a woman with pink hair and purple eyes. Franklin knew that the woman wasn't an Amazonas; that could only mean she was a soldier.

"What do you want?"

"We want to start a war."

"You're all insane." Franklin muttered.

"We've been told that by your kind." The warrior laughed again as the lights on Franklin's dash lit up. The driver hit every button he could but the Githraki had somehow taken control of the iguana-tron.

"What's going on?" Franklin snapped.

"Colony HQ, are you there?" The Githraki spoke in perfect imitation of Franklin's voice.

"*Yes.*" The response was immediate.

"Good," Franklin could detect humor in the Githraki's voice, "can you record a message?"

"*Yes...*" The reply was much more hesitant.

"Start recording," there was a brief pause, "now." Franklin tried everything he knew, but the Githraki had bypassed his control.

"For too long have humans tried to dominate the universe that they have no right too; but that time has changed. The Githraki stand against you, in this world and the world you come from, because humans have no place among the stars. For too long have humans tried to steal what does not belong to them; but that time has changed. The Githraki stand united against you, shoulder-to-shoulder with all the species around the universe, because humans are not welcome. We wage war on you to protect what we hold dear; prepare for doom."

A red light on the dash in front of Franklin began to blink rapidly. He knew what to expect as the blinking increased in speed. There was a sudden beeping sound and Franklin closed his eyes.

The iguana-tron exploded in a ball of blue flame, its nuclear capacitors ignited.

28

Caroline reclined in her seat as the recorded video played. It was a security video taken at the same time as the Githraki recording was sent, taken from the iguana-tron before it exploded.

"For too long have humans tried to dominate the universe that they have no right too; but that time has changed. The Githraki stand against you, in this world and the world you come from, because humans have no place among the stars. For too long have humans tried to steal what does not belong to them; but that time has changed. The Githraki stand united against you, shoulder-to-shoulder with all the species around the universe, because humans are not welcome. We wage war on you to protect what we hold dear; prepare for doom."

As the words played, Caroline focused on the imagery. She could see the tall, gaunt form of a Githraki warrior in the distance. It took some time and careful manipulation, but she'd been able to see Candy strapped to the hovering platform. She closed her eyes and let out a deep breath as the door to the room opened.

Alyssa walked in, her robotic eyes constantly adjusting as she swiveled her head around the room. Caroline kept the lights dim but not for any medical reason; she'd just grown fond of the darkness. Alyssa's eyes automatically allowed the sniper to view through the darkness; although the computer screens created odd shadows that tried to trick Alyssa's eyes.

"For too long have humans tried to dominate the universe that they have no right too; but that time has changed. The Githraki stand against you, in this world and the world you come from, because humans have no place among the stars. For too long have humans tried to steal what does not belong to them; but that time has changed. The Githraki stand united against you, shoulder-to-shoulder with all the species around the universe, because humans are not welcome. We wage war on you to protect what we hold dear; prepare for doom."

Caroline pressed a few buttons and the video replayed. The speakers replayed the Githraki's words while the woman closed her eyes. Alyssa sat in her assigned seat, though she suspected that her choice of seat was meaningless with most of the squad dead. Though she could watch the video, Alyssa was focused on Caroline.

"Sitting here can't be healthy," Alyssa whispered, "you should at least open the window blinds." Alyssa smiled weakly and started to stand when she heard the *click* of a gun's safety switch. Caroline had her pistol on her lap and aimed it at Alyssa, a single eye open.

"What do you want?" Caroline finally spoke.

"We survived Jurassic Earth," Alyssa raised her voice, "yet I'm the only one of us that seems eager to be alive."

"You've spent a lot of time and resources to improve your sniping talent," Caroline said as she holstered her pistol, "you should apply for a transfer so that you can get on a new Raptor."

"What would you do," Alyssa's eyes narrowed, "with me on another craft and John on one of the towers?" John had been approved for a temporary transfer to another part of the colony as general security. Despite her attempts, Caroline couldn't follow John; there was some red-tape that she wasn't able to cut through.

"Maybe I'll go back to the station," Caroline finally said, "perhaps I'll get to go back through ICARUS and serve on the Moon again."

"Will you do anything to avoid your former squad members?"

"I'm not avoiding you." Caroline whispered.

"You'll get your wish," Alyssa slowly got to her feet, "I'm going out with another Raptor in the morning. I was hoping to convince you to sign-up. Tolburn wants us to intimidate the Githraki," Alyssa explained, "and Holderson wants to impress upon the Githraki the power of the colony."

"You're going to be part of a firing squad, then?"

"You heard that recording," Alyssa frowned, "the Githraki have declared war on us. We'll stop them before they doom us or the Amazonas." She stood and took a step toward the door, her back turned to Caroline for a moment. She turned back after a second and

focused her eyes on Caroline. "You're not the only one of us that lost."
She left Caroline in the dark. The seconds ticked by but Caroline didn't
move. She closed her eyes again but she could still see Candy's pained
face.

The words echoed in John's head as he stared off into the distance.
He didn't mind what was happening; there was mild liberation in the
results. Without the fear of starting a family, Caroline had assured John
of that, John held no allegiance to his former squad. He took a deep
breath but continued to watch the horizon.

From his perch, John could see hundreds of Raptors slowly rise
from the landing platforms to intercept the Githraki army. The words
played over and over in John's head.

*"For too long have humans tried to dominate the universe that they
have no right too; but that time has changed. The Githraki stand against
you, in this world and the world you come from, because humans have no
place among the stars. For too long have humans tried to steal what does
not belong to them; but that time has changed. The Githraki stand united
against you, shoulder-to-shoulder with all the species around the universe,
because humans are not welcome. We wage war on you to protect what we
hold dear; prepare for doom."*

Holderson said it was important to memorize the threat, though
John didn't think that it was necessary.

"Are you planning to come in soon?" John's communicator blinked
red as the tower commander's voice was transmitted to him. John
tapped the communicator so that he could speak.

"Yeah." John had been sitting on the roof of the tower, able to
breathe the Jurassic air without fear of injury or death. But his place
was inside the tower with the other security soldiers. It was boring but
kept him away from Caroline and Alyssa. He'd been told that Caroline
had made several attempts to transfer to the same location, though
Holderson had stopped her attempts as John had requested.

John hopped down from the sloped tower roof and landed on the outer catwalk with grace. He watched the Raptors rise into the sky for a final moment before turning to go inside. He didn't see Alyssa in one of the Raptors; though she saw him.

Alyssa watched John turn to the tower, a dark figure against plate steel, and vanish through a glass door. She idly thumbed the trigger of the rifle as her concentration wavered. Part of her wanted to go back while part of her wanted to stay on the Raptor.

"Patel," the squad leader was a thorn in Alyssa's side, "pay attention!" Patel thought about slapping the muscled man but she was too busy keeping tabs on her former squad-mates.

"Sir; yes sir!" Alyssa said, loud enough to hear.

"That's better," the squad commander relaxed back to his own seat, "but keep an eye out; I heard about your last squad and I don't want to be killed like them."

"They're not all dead."

"Not physically," he sighed, "but they're all emotionally dead." Alyssa thought that Caroline was behaving in a similar fashion, but she didn't say anything as the Raptor's nose dipped and the craft flew over the jungle.

29

"What is a dinosaur?" McNeil paced in front of the crowd of new arrivals. They were standing in the outer-training yard; electrified fences buzzing, dinosaurs ignoring them. "That really depends on who you ask. Dinosaurs are animals; they vary in size but should always be treated with respect. Some dinosaurs, like the Ceratosaurus behind me, are flesh-eaters while some like Stegosaurus are herbivorous. Your personal computers are capable of identifying most species that you could encounter in the field; but distance from the colony decreases the effectiveness of the computer.

"I'm sure that if we decided to stick around for a few million years, we'd be able to determine how dinosaurs went extinct. But these animals are not bones; they are nature's weapon.

"This place looks like Earth once did, but it's not in the same dimension and not everything is guaranteed to happen. In Earth's history, mammals should've appeared but that hasn't happened. The only mammals you'll ever have the misfortune of encountering are Githraki..." His voice drifted off as he looked down to his feet. "We are on the brink of war with the Githraki," he looked up at the soldiers, "our survival means their defeat."

The Raptors reached the river like a cloud of thirsty insects, a dark mass made from thousands of flying crafts. There were no visible dinosaurs so the Raptors continued. Alyssa saw the place that her former squad's Raptor had crashed, forced out of the skies. The Raptor she was on didn't stop; it continued forward with the rest of the Raptors.

Soon, the wreckage of the iguana-tron was below. Every soldier on every Raptor could see the carnage: burnt metal was strewn around the edge of a grassy clearing. The ground was singed and the bodies of two large dinosaurs were nearby.

"*The Githraki have declared war*," the voice of Governor Tolburn went through every communicator, "*by word and by destroying a valuable machine. You're all cleared to go weapons-hot.*" The communicators clicked off as the soldiers unlocked their weapons. There was no sign of the Githraki in the area; Alyssa knew that they were still some distance away.

Without warning, a Raptor on the fringe of the convoy erupted in a ball of flames. As the craft fell to the jungle, a missile screamed through the air at another Raptor. The craft exploded as the missile made contact; everyone inside died. The Raptors broke formation as more missiles flew into the sky. The air was filled with the screams of death as a Raptor moved in Alyssa's direction. The Raptor was trying to avoid a missile as it moved to crash into another Raptor.

"I wish I wasn't here." Alyssa whispered. The Raptors collided and both turned into burning balls of flame.

Tolburn sat in the comfort of his office and watched the video monitors. The live-feed, sent from one of the Raptors, showed the mayhem that had begun as soon as the Raptors passed over the fallen iguana-tron. He watched until a missile hit the Raptor and the screen went black.

He slammed his fist on the desktop and cringed as his blood dripped from his fingers. With his other hand, he reached for the communicator and dialed Holderson.

"*Sir?*"

"This thing with the Githraki is getting old," Tolburn wrapped his bleeding hand in his shirt, "I need to send a squad out to bolster our defenses."

"*Sir; all of the active squads from the colony were sent out in the Raptors.*"

"What about inactive squads? What about all of those new soldiers that just arrived?"

"*Colony defense,*" Holderson replied softly, "*is not suitable for the task you need. If you let me lead something...*"

"I want a squad to go out, not your blood-bath of desire. What can be done?"

"*I suppose...*" Holderson paused. "*No, that's impossible.*"

"Nothing is impossible."

"*The remaining part of West's squad is likely available,*" Holderson suggested, "*Although I don't know how many of them are alive.*"

"Are they in the colony?"

"*They'd better be,*" Holderson's response was immediate, "*Scout Deacon is stationed in the South Tower while Squad-leader West is scheduled to return to the station.*"

"Is that it?"

"*Sir.*" Caroline and John were the only known remaining survivors of the squad.

"Can they be trusted?"

"*They were both part of a colony HQ squad until their...accident.*" Holderson was amused by the idea of using John's excuse.

"I want them in my office," Tolburn growled, "now!"

Caroline dressed in her old blue Naval uniform; form fitting with a golden star over her left breast. She'd had her hair trimmed so that she echoed the expected appearance of all Navy officers. She gave herself a quick examination in the mirror of her small room before she walked out into the hall. She knew that, once she'd walked away, she was never walking back to that same hall.

"Caroline West?" A pair of men in black uniforms similar to her own uniform stopped Caroline in the hall. She noticed that the men wore white gloves and had black berets on. Only one of the men spoke but both frightened her.

"Yes?"

"Colony Peace," the speaking man said, "can you come with us?"

"What's this about?" She looked at both men in turn but neither wanted to answer her question.

"Come with us."

John walked from the tower to the colony building. Not having to worry about wearing a breathing mask, he was able to take his time and enjoy the late afternoon air. He slowed and looked at the sky. The Raptors hadn't returned; John hoped that everything was alright.

John reached the building and a green door that allowed him entry. He pulled the handle and entered a narrow hall with a short descending staircase. He was near the communications center but John had no reason to go into those rooms. He was bound for his own residence; located in the building's basement.

His progress was stopped when a pair of men in black uniforms walked up the stairs. They wore white gloves and berets.

"Excuse me." John said, trying to be polite.

"Are you John Deacon?" One of the men asked while the other remained silent but solid.

"Who's asking?"

"Colony Peace," the speaker said, "are you John Deacon?"

"Yes." He didn't have any reason to lie.

"Come with us, please." John nodded and let the men lead him away. They didn't go very far; the peace officers brought John to the colony offices. They stopped in the main entranceway while John walked inside alone. Faces turned in his direction and John instinctively looked away. The secretary at the front of the office glanced up from behind her high desk but said nothing as John passed.

He turned to his left, not entirely paying attention to his direction, when he bumped into McNeil. The soldier stood with his arms crossing his chest as though he wanted to appear bigger; though that was unlikely to ever happen.

"How're the skies?" McNeil asked.

"Experience tells me that they're Hell," John shrugged, "but they appear calm."

"Do you miss the field?"

"I wasn't out there long enough to miss it."

"I'm speaking in general terms."

John shrugged his shoulders. "Sure." He paused. "What's this about?" John leaned closer to McNeil and spoke in a whisper.

"Did you see the Raptors leaving?" McNeil asked.

"Yes." John nodded.

"Did you see the Raptors returning?"

"No." John frowned.

"That's because the Githraki attacked the Raptors," McNeil explained, "all are presumed dead."

"Jesus…" John felt his mouth go dry. "But that doesn't explain what I'm doing here."

"The Governor requested your squad."

"Most of them are dead."

"He just wants to see the known survivors."

"That'd be me," John paused, "Alyssa, and Caroline."

"Alyssa Patel was on one of those Raptors that were destroyed." John heard McNeil but his mind was lost in thought, entirely forgetting that she was only 'presumed' to be dead..

"Oh…" John wondered how he was expected to react.

"Come on." McNeil held a hand to John and they walked into Tolburn's office together. Caroline turned her head and looked over her shoulder when McNeil led John into the room. She sighed and turned away.

"Great."

30

The jungle was coated by a thin layer of mist but that didn't deter anyone. The survivors from the fallen Raptors looked around but weren't comfortable so far from the Colony. They were careful to keep their face masks secured to their skin while eyeing the prehistoric jungle for threats. Any animal was a threat, even the small dinosaurs that scurried through the darkness. As the mist obscured their vision, the survivors activated the thermal scanners on their HUDs. The Heads-Up-Displays allowed the soldiers to have a level of calm, but their fingers still shook as they looked nervously around.

"Keep the line tight!" Alyssa growled, her own mask's communicator made conversation easier. She swept her rifle around in half-circles, eye always forward. Unlike the other survivors, she wasn't sweating; her technological eyes didn't require her to utilize thermal-imaging.

"We've got movement," one of the survivors near the end of the line called out, "a hundred yards out; closing fast!" The nervous man stopped walking and raised his rifle. He took a deep breath and clicked the safety switch on the side of the rifle.

From the jungle burst a small group of dinosaurs, less than half a dozen; small carnivores roughly four to five feet in length, the smallest were just over two feet long. They were too small to hunt humans.

"What are they?" One of the survivors asked.

"The computer is out of range," another survivor answered, "there's no way to tell."

"They eat meat," Alyssa said, "look at the claws. Also, notice the patterns on their scales; they ambush their prey from hiding."

"How do you know?"

"Just a guess, I suppose." Alyssa smiled.

"Why were they running?" The survivors were all nervous as Alyssa shifted her position so that she'd be covered by a fallen tree.

"There's still movement in front of us!" The first survivor cried out as an Allosaurus exploded from the foliage. The survivor opened fire but he was unable to stop the hungry dinosaur. He was caught in the Allosaurus' jaws and lifted into the air. The carnivore's powerful neck muscles easily lifted the human and shook him, breaking his bones before throwing his ragged body back to the ground. The dinosaur stopped and bent down so that it could eat its kill, breaking through the MKII like the shell of a crustacean.

"Allosaurs hunt in packs..." Alyssa whispered to herself; the other survivors were too scared to listen anyway. As the frightened humans ran, other Allosaurs appeared. One Allosaurus bent its head low so that a running human tripped over its head. The dinosaur lifted its head quickly and flipped the human into the air. Another Allosaurus moved quickly and snatched the flailing human out of the air. The human was bitten in half as he fell, his torso taken by one Allosaur while the one that flipped him took his legs. The body snapped apart as wires and entrails dangled together.

A fourth Allosaurus appeared and, using its powerful legs, jumped at a running human. Its claws sank into the human's back as the carnivore's teeth tore into his flesh. The frightened man cried out in horror before his scream faltered. Alyssa closed her eyes and sank into a fern beside the fallen tree. The Allosaurs hadn't noticed her and she took the opportunity to run.

She felt bad about leaving her comrades behind; but she knew that they'd all be dead soon enough.

"Great." Caroline looked away from John and slumped in her chair. John took a deep breath as McNeil turned him toward the seat beside Caroline, facing the Governor's desk. John moved reluctantly, taking each step slowly, until he was standing beside the chair. He looked at Caroline but, not knowing what to say, sat down in silence.

McNeil went to a chair in front of a row of windows where Holderson was already sitting. McNeil crossed his ankles and leaned back as much as his chair would allow and tried to relax; though he was already aware that the situation wasn't very relaxing.

"We've got trouble." Tolburn walked into the office, as silently as a cat. But without showing himself to either Caroline or John, he spoke. The soldiers turned to see a grim face, tired from stress, staring back.

"What happened?" Caroline asked.

"At 0800 hours, a fleet of Raptors were dispatched to quell the Githraki threat," Tolburn slowly walked to his desk and traced an invisible line against the surface, "but the Raptors were attacked."

"Was it an aerial predator?" John asked, thinking back to the crash his squad had gone through.

"We're not exactly sure what happened," Tolburn sighed, "but; we suspect that it was a missile attack." He fixed his eyes with Holderson.

"Our intel suggests that a Githraki army has formed in the nearby Amazonas camp." Holderson spoke softly.

"What do you want from us?" Caroline asked.

"The Raptors were destroyed and most of the soldiers killed," Tolburn ignored Caroline for the moment, "but the computers showed that there were a few survivors...and then the Raptors were all gone and we learned nothing else."

"What happened to the survivors?" Caroline asked.

"Personal CPUs are only effective at short distances from any relay tower or transport," Tolburn explained though Caroline already knew, "the survivors couldn't access their computers once the Raptors were destroyed."

"We suspect that all communication soldiers were killed," Holderson interrupted, "since they carry stronger CPUs than regular soldiers."

"The communication office has been working since the Raptors were destroyed to get us some information. They said it was hard work but," he tapped a few keys on a hidden keyboard, "they got something." Tolburn wanted to smile but he was unable.

"We've ... movement ... closing fast!" Tolburn had the audio recording replayed several times but it was clear to everyone that something had happened to the survivors.

"Was Alyssa among the survivors?" John asked. Caroline looked at John but said nothing.

"We don't know who survived." Tolburn said.

"I had Patel assigned as a door-gunner," Holderson said, "so it's possible."

"Even if she survived the attack on the Raptors," Tolburn said, "there's no guarantee that she survived the jungle."

"She's been in that Hell before," John said, "I think that she'll be fine."

"You never told us what you want from us." Caroline said, changing the subject so that she could stop thinking about Alyssa.

"You're right," Tolburn sighed, "your... talents... may be useful to us."

"Talents?" Caroline asked.

"Experience." Tolburn corrected himself.

"What does that mean?"

"The pair of you survived a devastating Raptor crash, survived as prisoners of the Githraki and Amazonas, and even managed to return to the Colony relatively unharmed."

"Not all of us returned." Caroline bowed her head.

"I'm aware of that," Tolburn reached for a file on his desk and opened it to the front page, "Rachel Gutierrez did not return and remains as a prisoner of the Githraki; she was showed to us in a taunt."

"Then you're also aware that we don't like to leave anyone behind." John hissed.

"Sacrifices must be made." Holderson murmured. Caroline looked at Holderson with fire in her eyes.

"I won't sacrifice Candy to those monsters!" Caroline snapped.

"What I need," Tolburn interrupted before a fight exploded in the office, "are you two to head to the relay station a mile outside of our perimeter. It will be the first place reached by the Githraki army and must not be destroyed." John leaned forward in his seat.

"Why is it so important? Can't relay stations be rebuilt?" John asked. His vision changed so that he could watch Tolburn's body temperature. Tolburn remained calm and his color didn't change, but his heart was racing and growing hotter. John knew that a lie was coming.

"We want to communicate with our soldiers that far from the Colony." Tolburn said softly.

"Don't lie to us." John said without hesitation.

"I'm not lying."

"Yes, you are."

"It doesn't matter to a grunt like you," Tolburn squared his shoulders. John could see him sweating, "just do as you're told."

"Tell us the truth or let the relay station burn." Caroline said as she crossed her arms.

"I..." Tolburn paused and dropped his head, "There are plans for that relay station. Several relay stations, in point of fact, but that one station will be vital to the future of this colony."

"How vital can a relay station be," Caroline's eyes narrowed, "especially when it could be rebuilt."

"The gate to be constructed in the Githraki settlement will require a lot of power that this colony cannot supply. A reactor is going to be built to the East but the power needs to be transported without passing through the Colony," Tolburn sighed, "the necessary relay stations are going to be retrofit with converters for transporting nuclear energy."

"Nuclear?" Caroline sat up in her seat.

"Nuclear energy caused World War III," John nearly jumped out of his own seat, "and you want to bring it here? That garbage cost us half of North America!"

"With the Githraki eliminated, there won't be any threat to the reactor," Tolburn tried to quiet Caroline and John, "but the power is too extensive for the Colony to handle. Until a better system can be devised, the relay stations are our best option." Tolburn looked from John to Caroline and smiled.

31

Alyssa pushed a frond aside and looked up to the sky; the narrow tip of the relay tower wasn't far. She found a smile, the first she had since the Raptors fell from the air, and stepped forward. With her rifle slung over her left shoulder, she began to walk the last mile to the relay station.

She paused once when she heard a roar in the distance, but she was confident that she'd proceed unimpeded. A few herbivores, including a nearby Stegosaurus, ate calmly. Alyssa watched the seen and saw an infant Stegosaurus jogging around the adult for scraps without a care in the Jurassic world. Alyssa moved on; confident.

Jürgen stood in the center of the village, his arms folded behind his back, as a cart was rolled out to him. Village priests, heads hidden under large hoods, bowed and departed in silence. A Githraki general, dressed in a splendorous cloak with red eyes and emerald green skin, had all four arms crossed in front of his large chest while Jürgen yelled commands in the 'German' language common to the Amazonas.

"Perfekt, wird sie in die Knie zwingen." Jürgen opened the box on the cart and removed the device inside. It looked like a silver box with several buttons on top of it. Githraki writing on the silver surface told Jürgen what the box would do. He cradled the box like a newborn infant and turned to look at the woman crouched nearby. Dressed in the rags that Jürgen had seen fit to give her, the woman known as 'Candy' was dirty and her colorful hair was leeched with black streaks.

"What're you going to do?" Candy asked. Though it wasn't allowed in Amazonas culture, Colony women spoke out of turn.

The Githraki general smiled. "We plan to use this device to enslave the 'Utahraptors' that hide in this region."

"What's a Utahraptor?" Candy asked while tears streamed down her face. Whatever it was, she knew it would be bad.

"In a place called Utah, eventually near this area, a dinosaur will be found. Though thought to only exist in the future, they exist in this time where they are elusive and rare.

"The Utahraptor is large and horrible," the Githraki clicked as though it was reciting from memory, "with a curved neck and hooked claws on the middle toe; they hunt in packs to bring down larger herbivores. They are fast runners and strong jumpers; highly intelligent."

"It sounds like that old movie we were made to watch before coming here." Candy muttered.

"Your people will suffer," Jürgen said with a smile, "I will burn them to the ground a step at a time. Between here and your colony is a tower of metal, a symbol of your influence on the land. We will send the Utahraptors against it and let the world tear the steel down."

He laughed as Candy wrapped her arms around her legs and tried to shrink into nothing.

The four-wheeled all-terrain vehicle, nicknamed the Hog, forced its way through the jungle along a dirt road that was hardly visible. Its four wheels bumped along the path over jutting rocks with nothing to absorb the shocking impacts on the passengers. The Hog's driver, Ted Samson, tried to avoid all of the pits and ditches but it was still a bumpy ride. Caroline, sitting in the front passenger seat, held on to the curved rolling cage as the Hog bounced along.

"This road will eventually be paved," Samson said in a Southern White City accent, "once the new gate is built. But those damn Githraki are holding us back." His voice was transmitted through the voice transmitter on his throat.

"Watch the road." Caroline snapped as she noticed the Hog swerving toward the brush on the narrow road. At the last moment, the vehicle darted away from the encroaching bushes. Samson was laughing.

"Too close for comfort, eh?" He continued to laugh as he looked in his rearview mirror at John. "How're ye holdin' up back there?"

"Are we there yet?" John was looking in the mirror with narrow eyes; it unnerved Samson. The driver immediately looked away.

"Just a few more minutes, sweetheart," Samson looked back at the dirt road, "just-"

A figure stepped into the road, face mask obscuring her face. She had a colony rifle shouldered which could be converted to a sniper rifle. She was hunched over and her MKII was dirty. The figure stumbled forward, eyes on the nearby relay tower, and stopped in the Hog's path.

"Hog One-Oh-Eight to Colony HQ." Samson radioed as he slammed on the brakes. The Hog stopped a few yards from the stranger who finally noted the vehicle.

"*Go ahead.*" The response was immediate. While all of the Hog's passengers could hear the communication, only Samson was connected to the HQ.

"I've spotted a human figure dressed in an MKII suit," Samson said as he eyed the stranger, "any advice?"

"*Make contact with the human and get identification,*" there was a pause, "*you have authorization to eliminate any threat that you encounter.*"

"Ten-four," Samson clicked a switch on the dashboard and the communication range increased so that the stranger could be spoken too, "stranger; identify yourself or be fired upon."

"Don't shoot," a female voice spoke weakly, "I cannot reach my weapon." The stranger was clearly human and not just humanoid.

"Who are you?"

"Alyssa Patel, sniper and Raptor door-gunner." She had her arms raised and was facing the Hog. Caroline leaned forward in her seat while John turned his head to look at Alyssa's ragged form.

"The radio broadcast said that all active Raptors were destroyed," Samson said, "with no survivors." John looked away.

"That's a lie," Alyssa replied, "I can prove it." She paused. When she spoke, everyone in the Hog could understand her. "Colony computer: voice recognition."

"*Please hold... please hold... please hold,*" there was a short moment of silence, "*Patel, Alyssa; Number 3060706010; West Squad; Stationed at CHQ.*"

"Is that good enough for you?" Alyssa asked Samson.

"Is that really you?" Caroline whispered.

"I could use a ride." Alyssa heard Caroline but didn't respond to her. Her focus was on Samson and, while looking, noticed John without saying a word.

Tolburn ran to the desk and stood beside the communications officer while pulling the radio in his direction. He looked at the computer screen in front of him that was displaying Alyssa's information.

"Patel, is that you?" Tolburn asked.

"*Sir, yes sir.*" The reply was quick and strong. Tolburn knew that each Hog carried medical supplies that every soldier was trained to use. Alyssa was important; as a member of Caroline West's former squad and a skilled sniper, Alyssa was an asset that nobody wanted to throw away.

"It's good to have you back."

32

The Hog pulled into the garage under the relay tower. Samson pulled the vehicle to a pair of sliding doors while the passengers watched. Alyssa sat next to John but she didn't touch him; Caroline pretended that she was alone in the vehicle. Samson casually looked at all of his passengers but only addressed Caroline.

"I have to return to HQ," Samson said, "I'll just drop you all off here."

"Fine." Caroline mumbled as the Hog came to a stop. The doors slid open but nobody was present to welcome the new arrivals. Caroline stepped out of the vehicle while John and Alyssa were forced to climb out of the back.

"See ya'll soon." Samson smiled and waved before leaving. Nobody spoke but Caroline nodded and led the way through the sliding doors. The doors closed when the new arrivals had passed and a flashing sign indicated that they could remove their face masks. The soldiers did as indicated, removing their masks and sliding them into the pouches they wore.

"Welcome to Relay Station AY-EX-One," a voice announced over a hidden PA system, "I regret that I cannot greet you in person but I'm occupied with other matters. Please wait for me in the common room at the end of the hall." The speaker was a man and spoke like a bureaucrat. The PA system went silent.

A door at the end of the hall opened and the three humans decided, silently, to go to the open door. They entered the common room, a green room with three couches arranged in a half-circle and a low table between them. Caroline sat in the center couch while John and Alyssa took the other two. They didn't speak for several seconds.

John let his vision change and turned his attention to Caroline. Able to see her body temperature, John noticed that Caroline's heart was racing while Alyssa had the body of a calm person.

John noticed something else about Caroline that made his own heart stop.

Another door opened and entered a bald man wearing a grey suit with a white ID tag hanging from his lapel. He had a smile on as he walked to the front of the room. His tag identified him as Russell Stewart.

"Welcome to Relay Station AY-EX-One," Russell said as sweat dripped from his brow. John noticed that the man's face was red and a deeper look revealed temperature extremes, "Governor Tolburn told me what your purpose is."

"What purpose is that?" Alyssa asked. Russell looked at her and his smile faltered for an instant.

"You're to defend this station from the Githraki threat," Russell said, "since this is the station closest to the Githraki army."

"What were you doing before you came to see us?" John asked. He could see that Russell was still flustered.

"I was in a meeting," Russell said, "that couldn't be interrupted." John frowned at Russell's lie but said nothing else. "Are there any additional questions, or can we begin the tour?"

The relay station was primarily unoccupied as it currently acted as a relay point for the computer; but there was evidence of construction as the station was going to be retrofitted to pass nuclear energy. The living quarters and offices were located in an underground bunker with a small work station of dials and buttons just above the ground.

Russell pressed a button in the residential hall and a door slid open. He walked into a room less than ten-feet square. He turned to face the soldiers with a grim smile.

"Unfortunately, proper quarters could not be constructed in time for your arrival. We were lucky to get this bunk constructed once we learned that there would be three soldiers arriving," the room was bare except for three small beds; two stacked against one wall and the third against the opposite wall, "the two women can sleep in these beds while the single man can sleep in this bed." Russell indicated which beds would be occupied by whom; John would be separated from Caroline and Alyssa by a few feet.

"I think that I speak for everyone," John said, "when I say that this space is too small for us. We'd prefer three rooms to avoid complications."

"What complications?"

"We don't get along very well." Caroline spoke before John could say the same thing.

"I'm sorry; but this is the best that we could do in such short time," Russell frowned, "you'll have to learn to share." Russell stepped out of the room while the three soldiers examined their new space. They didn't seem pleased and Caroline pursed her lips as she dropped her duffel bag on the bottom bunk.

"How long will it be until we get new quarters?" John asked.

"It could be as soon as a few days," Russell shrugged, "or as long as a few weeks."

"Are there going to be three rooms?" Caroline asked, hopeful, as she looked at Russell.

"Sorry," Russell flashed a false smile, "but only two rooms were ordered. We did not expect a third person so you two women will have to share a room once it arrives."

"We have a history that," Caroline searched for the right words, "doesn't favor sharing."

"I am truly sorry," Russell bowed, "but I've done all I could." He looked at the three soldiers in turn but no longer smiled. "The mess is down the hall, the bathrooms are spaced through the residential rooms. Dinner will be served in an hour."

"Thanks." Alyssa mumbled.

"The bathrooms are fitted with showers for your use." Russell noted the grime on Alyssa's clothes.

"That's appreciated."

Russell bowed again and the door slid shut, separating him from the three soldiers. He walked and disappeared into the nearest bathroom while the three soldiers took stock of their room.

"How long before we kill each other?" Caroline asked.

"I don't know," Alyssa looked at Caroline, "are you intending to poison us?"

"What're you talking about?" Caroline's hand rested on her pistol but it was still secured to her belt.

"I had a blood test taken after we left the hyperbolic chamber," Alyssa's eyes narrowed, "a poisonous concoction was present in my system..."

"Are you accusing me of something?"

"I'm saying that you tried to kill me," Alyssa rested her hand on her own pistol, "and you failed; I don't think that you're the sort of woman that fails *twice*."

"I did it with the best intentions." Caroline slid the pistol from the holster and held it at her waist, aiming at the floor.

"I'm a better shot that you." Alyssa drew her own pistol and aimed at Caroline.

"Enough of this!" John snapped a moment before he moved. His motions were a blur as he grabbed the pistols from Caroline and Alyssa. He tossed them behind himself so that they landed on his bunk. The two women looked at John with wide eyes as John's spine grew unnoticed under his armor.

"What happened to you?" Caroline whispered as she looked at John. "What did the Githraki do to you?"

John didn't reply.

33

The spotter stood on a platform constructed halfway up the relay tower. He was short and barely able to look above the railing, but he still had the lonely job above the station. He yawned and continued to watch the jungle though it was impossible to pierce the dense foliage.

"*Spotter.*" The man's radio crackled; it was the station calling.

"Go ahead."

"*The computer has detected movement in the jungle at one-two-six; can you confirm?*"

"Wait a second," he tried to remember where one-two-six was before moving into position. He scanned the jungle but noticed nothing, "I've got eyes on the jungle but I can't spot anything."

"*Keep an eye out.*"

"No problem." He frowned and continued watching. *Dumb bitch*, he thought to himself, *all my job requires is that I keep an eye out.* He sighed and looked through the binoculars attached to his helmet.

The brush near the edge of the jungle rattled as a dinosaur leapt into view. The spotter leaned forward, though his motions were restricted by the railing, and tried to get a closer look.

"Computer, can you identify?" He spoke.

"*Please hold... please hold... please hold...*" there was a moment of silence before the computer replied to him, "*classification: Utahraptor. Bipedal theropod that is thought to hunt in packs. Only known to exist during the early Cretaceous period, though some paleontologists have argued that they also existed during the Jurassic period.*"

"I think that I can prove those paleontologists right," he said with a smile before his eyes narrowed, "did you say it was a pack hunter?"

"*Yes.*"

"I see only one," he frowned, "where's the rest of the pack?" His question was answered as he heard a thump on the platform nearby. He turned to see the hissing maw of a six-foot long Utahraptor. It was crouched but didn't lunge.

Another Utahraptor landed on the opposite side of the platform, forcing the man to turn. He was practically surrounded with nowhere to go. He started to cry.

His tears were ended when a bullet bore a hole through his head. He collapsed, dead, on the platform while the Utahraptors watched. With their minds enslaved, they couldn't resist the command given to them.

"What is this supposed to be?" John asked as he sat down. He was forced to sit with Caroline and Alyssa because no other seat was available.

"Roast beef," Caroline said as she looked at the gray mush in the bowl, "though it'll probably taste like packing material." Her humor wasn't shared.

"Something's going on here," John stabbed the mystery meat with a plastic spork, "I know it."

"Russell was unnerved about something," Caroline nodded, "though I suppose that we're all a little on edge." She looked at John with narrow eyes.

"There's a difference between 'a little on edge' and lying." John was oblivious to Caroline's stare. She was continuing to look at him while she thought back to the night she became pregnant.

John had come to her, hours before he was supposed to relieve her. They had exchanged words; there was a brief talk about how they now saw the world with their masks gone, and then John confessed that he'd thought a lot about her over the past few years. She'd tried to remind John that he was still mourning the unfortunate death of his wife and son, and then he kissed her. It was a deep, passionate kiss. He lifted her off the ground and slammed her into the tree she had been sitting against. Caroline didn't know who undressed first; she didn't remember the small details. All she remembered was John.

Then, when she returned to camp, she thought about the future: life would be Hell if she was pregnant. She had cried herself to sleep while Alyssa had watched.

"It's not our place to worry about the details," Alyssa said, "our job is to protect the Colony from all threats; in and out." She saw Caroline and spoke before she could say anything. John, still oblivious to Caroline, nodded.

"Who was he meeting with?" John wondered.

"It doesn't matter." Alyssa looked at Caroline.

"John, you-" Caroline started to growl when John grabbed the top of her head with his right hand and pulled her head to the tabletop. John pulled Alyssa's head down and leaned forward as a small rocket burst through the open door and exploded a wall. A few nearby construction workers died in the unexpected blast.

"Humans die!" John heard a war-cry and growled; not because it was a Githraki but because the cry came from *within* the station's halls: that meant the Githraki had been allowed to enter.

The hall outside of the mess hall was filled with a white smoke that clung to clothing, like the smoke from a fire yet there was no fire. John, able to see clearly, saw the holes in the hallway's walls and cringed.

"The walls are open." Alyssa, with her robotic-enhanced eyes, gasped at what she saw. Human soldiers unaccustomed to the rich Jurassic oxygen were scrambling to put their masks on while Caroline's broken squad marched ahead; Caroline and Alyssa absently clicked their masks shut. The three soldiers, alone, walked out of the tower and stopped when they saw the breadth of the Githraki army. Mingling among the green and brown Githraki warriors were local Amazonas; one had a battered Candy Gutierrez at the end of a chain.

"What do you want?" Caroline asked in the best diplomatic voice she could muster.

"Your plans have been told to us," the Githraki general clicked its mandibles in joy, "now the time has come for humans to die!" He started to move but John was faster.

In a single, swift motion; John dropped to one knee and raised his rifle. Before the Githraki general could even raise his own weapon, John pulled the trigger. Three white beams struck the Githraki general in the chest an instant before a large pulse ripped its chest open.

The Githraki started to open fire randomly, laser blasts hitting structure and ally alike as a pair of missile platforms unleashed fury on the relay station. A pair of large dinosaurs rushed from the obscure sides of the relay station. The dinosaur opened their mouths, unleashing horrify shrieks, and jumped with claws raised in the air. John drew the dagger from his belt and threw it at one of the dinosaurs; he drew Caroline's dagger and threw it at the other. Both dinosaurs fell to the ground, twitching in death spasms, as some Githraki fled in fear.

"Humans... die!" The Amazonas holding Candy prisoner, dressed in the tattered remains of a US Airforce uniform, raised a hooked sword high above his head. With his muscular arm, born from ancestors strengthening their bodies and a culture of physical prowess, Jürgen cleaved Candy's head away from her body.

"No!" Caroline screamed as she raised her rifle. She pulled the trigger on her weapon and unleashed a fury of bullets into Jürgen's chest. The Amazonas fell to the ground, dead. John watched the blood pour from Candy's neck; her death was no accident, Jürgen had done it for fun. Caroline ran to the fallen soldier but John knew that it was pointless, Candy was clearly dead.

John took a step in the direction of the Githraki army and froze; he could smell a rotten odor that swept across the army. It was a smell that he recognized and feared. Githraki warriors halted and looked back: a pair of Allosaurs rushed out of the woods with their claws tearing into the closest Githraki warriors.

Another Allosaur ran out of the jungle with its head bowed, knocking several Githraki warriors off of their feet. A fourth Allosaur rushed the Gitghaki army from John's left, one of the Githraki's dinosaurs in its jaws, and grabbed a few unlucky warriors in its claws.

While the Githraki had a measure of protection created by their strong exoskeletons and thick bones, the Amazonas had nothing to protect them. The Githraki, in their attempt to escape death, threw Amazonas warriors at the Allosaurs. The massive dinosaurs didn't care.

Another Utahraptor, its eyes glazed over, jumped down from the catwalk tower with its jaws opened and claws raised for the kill. John turned and grabbed the hissing dinosaur by its neck and threw it to the ground. John's spine fully broke through his suit and a hooked spike from his back arched above John's head and impaled the Utahraptor in the dinosaur's left eye.

"Die!" John screamed. A second pair of arms burst from his chest and held the dinosaur's thrashing body away from his fragile form. Sparks from the remnants of his suit burned the dinosaur's flesh as it sprayed on the dead animal.

"John," Caroline rested a gloved hand on John's shoulder and the soldier looked at Caroline with red eyes, "John." John took several deep breaths and his heart slowed enough for his eyes to return to normal and the Githraki limbs retracted.

EPILOGUE

"Everything is going as planned," the creature watched the Githraki army crumble from a safe distance, "everything." It turned its binoculars until it saw John Deacon. "I think that the experiment has been a success." The creature smiled; its wide mouth flashing and its white teeth gleaming. It handed the binoculars to the armored man standing nearby.

"Sir," the man had to speak through a radio since he wore a mask to protect himself from the Jurassic air, "I have a question."

"Oh?" The creature shifted its bulbous, anthropomorphic body to look at the man.

"Why bother?"

"The Githraki have always been a threat to my people," the creature turned away, "and humans were a threat to the Githraki. Instigating a war between humans and the Githraki was an obvious choice to protect what I hold dear."

"Why this place? Why the Jurassic?"

"The humans were coming here; some unfortunate humans came here by accident, but they were always destined to come to this place. It was fortunate for my people; the Githraki-Human war in modern times had come to a stalemate, only a new war in this place and continued hatred between the two species could lead to the destruction of the Githraki threat." It laughed as a fifth Allosaur rushed into the Githraki ranks.

Don't miss out!

Visit the website below and you can sign up to receive emails whenever Michael Bertolini publishes a new book. There's no charge and no obligation.

https://books2read.com/r/B-A-EMBLB-FZZHD

BOOKS 2 READ

Connecting independent readers to independent writers.

Also by Michael Bertolini

Dark Heritage Saga
The Cold Tower; Dark Heritage Saga I
The Shadow Road; Dark Heritage Saga II
The Lost Worlds; Dark Heritage Saga III
The Keeper's Gate, Dark Heritage Saga IV
The Blood Fields, Dark Heritage Saga V
Wanderer

Horrorscope
Solitary
Behind the Veil
Creature Of The Night
For Rent
Interview
Leviathan
On A Quiet Stretch Of Road
Pale
Solar
Sonne
Somebody Please Help
The Soldier's Wife
The Thing That Should Have Remained Buried

Unwanted Room

Watch for more at www.michaeljbertolini.com.

Milton Keynes UK
Ingram Content Group UK Ltd.
UKHW020842030624
443491UK00013B/276